Sherlock Holmes:
Far & Wide

Nine Stories and One Play
Including the award-winning,
"Sir Arthur & The Time Machine."

Gretchen Altabef

Hardcover ISBN 978-1-80424-587-3
Paperback ISBN 978-1-80424-588-0
ePub ISBN 978-1-80424-589-7
PDF ISBN 978-1-80424-590-3

Published by MX Publishing
335 Princess Park Manor, Royal Drive,
London, N11 3GX
www.mxpublishing.co.uk

Cover design by Awan

Robida, Albert. *The Future Imagined*. La Vie Électrique. Image created for the Paris 1900 World Exposition. 1890.

Paget, Sidney. "The Reichenbach Fall". Arthur Conan Doyle, "The Adventure of the Final Problem", *The Strand Magazine*, London, UK. 1893.

Steele, Frederick Dorr. "My Collection Of M's Is A Fine One." Illustration for *Collier's Weekly Magazine*. Arthur Conan Doyle. "The Adventure of the Empty House." New York, US. 1903.

Peters, Charles. (1883). "The Crown Rose." Editor of monograph: *A Crown of Flowers, being poems and pictures collected from the pages of The Girl's Own Paper*. British Library digitised image shelfmark: "Digital Store 11602.gg.11." Religious Tract Society, London, UK. 1883.

Frankie, Gordon W; Thorp, Robbin W; Coville, Rollin E; Ertter, Barbara. *California Bees and Blooms*. Bee Anatomy Illustration. Heyday Books, Berkeley, CA, US. 2014.

Steele, Frederick Dorr. (1904). Paget, Sidney. (1892). "A Toast Darling." (By G. Altabef). Arthur Conan Doyle. "The Adventure of the Speckled Band." *The Strand Magazine*, London, UK. 1892. "The Adventure of the Golden Pince-Nez." *Collier's Weekly Magazine*, New York, US. 1904.

Steele, Frederic Dorr. "Sherlock Holmes in disguise." Arthur Conan Doyle, "The Adventure of Charles Augustus Milverton." Illustration for Collier's Weekly Magazine, New York, US. 1904.

Van Maële, Martin. Illustration of Irene Adler for "A Scandal In Bohemia." Arthur Conan Doyle. Société d'Édition et de Publications, Paris, France. 1905.

Atherton, Matt. 19th-Century Whaling. "Sperm Whales 'Swiftly Learned' To Evade Harpoons In Adaptation Move To Avoid Whalers." Express, Mar. 17, 2021. www.express.co.uk/

Steele, Frederic Dorr. "The Adventure Of Black Peter." Sir Arthur Conan Doyle. Illustrated for the cover of *Collier's Weekly Magazine*. 1904.

Steele, Frederic Dorr. "The one thing I don't know about it, you're going to tell me now, Holmes announced calmly." Arthur Conan Doyle, "The Adventure of the Mazarin Stone." Illustration for *Hearst's International Magazine*, New York, US. 1921.

Steele, Frederic Dorr. Illustration of Sherlock Holmes. Arthur Conan Doyle, "The Adventure of the Golden Pince-Nez." *Collier's Magazine*, New York, US. 1904.

Dedicated to Jack Altabef my favourite composer of no ordinary merit. Your melodies fill me with encouragement and love, your songs are my inspiration.

Table of Contents

All footnotes and explanations shall be found in Notes For Curious.

Sherlock Holmes by Fredrick Dorr Steele. [1]

Introduction

"The following stories paint Mr Sherlock Holmes and his activities upon a somewhat broader canvas where there is room for expansion. This expansion must express itself in action, for there is no room for character development in the conception of a detective. Whatever you add to the one central quality of astuteness must in my opinion detract from the general effect. Other writers may however succeed where I fail." Arthur Conan Doyle. [2]

Sherlock Holmes–Far And Wide is a compilation of my somewhat broader short stories and one play. Originally published separately in anthologies and now collected here for the reader. They are my attempts to succeed or continue where Sir Arthur Conan Doyle left off.

After all, the genre he perfected was followed by the Golden Age of Detective Fiction in the 1920s and 1930s. I doubt very much that Agatha Christie, Margery Allingham, or Dorothy L. Sayers would agree with Doyle's approach to characterisation. Even Raymond Chandler married off his hard-boiled detective Philip Marlowe in his last book. But then, again, Sherlock Holmes has entered his third century (1854 – 2024) awash in pastiches.

Like Doctor Doyle, I author mysteries for Sherlock Holmes to solve. And like Doctor Watson, I like nothing better than to associate myself with one of Holmes's adventures. And like Jeremy Brett, I explore the cracks in Holmes's marble. While historical research is how I run, the rest is improvisation. Written in grateful communication with the muse, each story evolves in its own way.

"I could not wish anything better than to be associated with my friend in one of those singular adventures which were the normal condition of his existence." The Man with the Twisted Lip.

Sherlockians and Holmesians who play "The Game" place Arthur Conan Doyle as Doctor Watson's literary agent, the stories as the factual biography of Mr Sherlock Holmes, and hold that both Holmes and Watson and everyone else in the sixty stories are real. As Conan Doyle stated at the very beginning of *A Study in Scarlet* and elsewhere, Doctor Watson is the author and he is a gracious host.

"Being a reprint from the reminiscences of John H. Watson M.D., late of the Army Medical Department." *A Study in Scarlet.*

"In glancing over my notes of the seventy odd cases in which I have during the last eight years studied the methods of my friend Sherlock Holmes, I find many tragic, some comic, a large number merely strange, but none commonplace; for, working as he did rather for the love of his art than for the acquirement of wealth, he refused to associate himself with any investigation which did not tend towards the unusual, and even the fantastic." The Adventure of the Speckled Band.

Throughout the chronicles of Sherlock Holmes, Doctor Watson seems that gentle-everyman who rises above his own expectations. In his honourable capacity to overtake himself, he stimulates the greatest mind of his day. With the courage of a soldier and wartime medic, the Doctor takes up his pen as a means to justice and sets the record straight.

"Your merits should be publicly recognized. You should publish an account of the case. If you won't, I will for you… I have all the facts in my journal, and the public shall know them." *A Study in Scarlet.*

"Boxing Day Brother Mine" is a holiday confection timed to exist in the middle of Sir Arthur Conan Doyle's short story, "The Adventure of the Blue Carbuncle." Sherlock brings his brother Mycroft into the heart of his dilemma. Mycroft's responses supply Sherlock with an alternative view of the problem. The Holmes Brothers play the game, relive their childhood adventures, and renew their friendly brotherhood for another year. Sherlock continues on in Doyle's story to solve the case and recover the one-of-a-kind gem, the Blue Carbuncle.

"Nothing clears up a case so much as stating it to another person." The Adventure of Silver Blaze.

When I'm deeply connected to the creativity and intuition that can nurture a story or novel, my muse materialises in dreams and I wake with dialogue in my ears. As an author, I wish nothing better than to share a similar awe with Doctor Watson.

A New York playwright taught me about this connection. Each day, she would arrive at rehearsal elaborately dressed as one of her characters, speak their lines in their accent, and sing and dance their numbers with the other actors. She taught by example and was fully in touch with her young company and the muse.

"Watson insists that I am the dramatist in real life," said he. "Some touch of the artist wells up within me and calls insistently for a well-staged performance. Surely our profession, Mr Mac, would be a drab and sordid one if we did not sometimes set the scene so as to glorify our results. The blunt accusation, the brutal tap upon the shoulder - what can one make of such a denouement? But the quick inference, the subtle trap, the clever forecast of coming events, the triumphant vindication of bold theories - are these not the pride and the justification of our life's work? At the present moment you thrill with the glamour of the situation and the anticipation of the hunter. Where would be that thrill if I had been as definite as a time-table?" *The Valley of Fear.*

What would you do? If you had the chance, would you travel to the future or the past? "Sir Arthur & The Time Machine" came to me as inspiration and invitation. What would Sir Arthur Conan Doyle do when faced with an actual functioning Time Machine? Without a second thought, he would jump into the future to solve his present dilemma. His search for answers led him first to his friend H. G. Wells.

Arthur Conan Doyle was an enormous soul. He was the hero of his life and a mighty adventurer. In medical school, he was assistant to the genius professor, Doctor Joseph Bell. Bell's unique form of diagnosis became through Doyle's imagination the celebrated method of his Great Detective.

"I thought of my old teacher Joe Bell, of his eagle face, of his curious ways, of his eerie trick of spotting details. If he were a detective he would surely reduce this fascinating but unorganized business to something nearer to an exact science. I would try if I could get this effect. It was surely possible in real life, so why should I not make it plausible in fiction? It is all very well to say that a man is clever, but the reader wants to see examples of it — such examples as Bell gave us every day in the wards [of Edinburgh Medical School]." *Memories And Adventures.* [3]

After graduating from medical school, and as he put it, receiving his medical "licence to kill," Doyle's first employment as a medic was with an Artic whaling crew. He served as Ship's Doctor for seven months.

"Never had such a jolly time in my life." Arthur Conan Doyle. [4]

He was an amateur boxer who loved a good fight, a cricketer who usually won the game for his team. Later, during the Boer War, he was deemed too old to enlist. Undaunted, he joined as a surgeon in a frontline hospital, wrote dispatches to *The Times*, and campaigned for better soldier protective gear.

At one time, Doctor Doyle opened a medical practice in Southsea, near Portsmouth. Here he set his story, "The Adventure of the Crooked Man." He knew of the regiment in Portsmouth, the town's streets, and its homes. As a local physician, he treated its residents and learned the town's secrets.

Many authors live varied or adventurous lives, like Doctor's Doyle and Watson. Ernest Hemingway's lived history amplified the reality in his novels. His interests were bullfighting, big game hunting, deep sea fishing, and newspaper reporting. During World War I, he drove an ambulance on the Italian front. Hemingway visited Spain during the Civil War and from this experience came *For Whom the Bell Tolls*.[5]

Likewise, for me, during the days of the "Son of Sam" murders in Brooklyn, New York, I worked in the locked wards of a Brooklyn psychiatric hospital. Where, following his arrest, the serial killer was incarcerated for psychological testing. Living through this terrifying time and those I met on the wards influenced the writing of my first novel, *These Scattered Houses*. That exposure filled the goings on at the historic Hudson Asylum with the authenticity of a witness.

> "I took to my heels, did ten miles over the mountains in the darkness, and a week later I found myself in Florence, with the certainty that no one in the world knew what had become of me." The Adventure of the Empty House.

"In The Land Of The Living" is my answer to this one sentence from Conan Doyle's story "The Adventure of the Empty House."

Doyle's directions lead Sherlock Holmes away from his Reichenbach battle with Professor Moriarty and Colonel Sebastian Moran's attacks. The story takes him through the high peaks of Switzerland on foot, by train and boat across Italy, steamship down the Suez Canal, training across India, and on horseback through the Nathu La Pass. Onward to the Tibetan Himalayas to save the life of a kidnapped boy, the thirteenth Dalai Lama.

> "As a rule, where historical novels fail is in the fact that there is too much history and too little novel. They want wakening up. Mr. Andrew Lang read *Micah Clarke* and

liked it. One man criticised it as having no plot, but a plot in an historical novel is an insult... It is the tournament, the battles that live. It is a mistake to take away the reader's eyes from the grand panorama." Sir Arthur Conan Doyle. [6]

Sherlock Holmes never shares what he knows unless he has validated it first. Conan Doyle followed his trusty ordnance map of London, as I did. Here, he gave us a snapshot of how he reconstructed the language of the fourteenth century for his novel, *The White Company*.

> "Well, of course, I am not archaeologically correct; I now and again threw in a Chaucerian word to give, as it were, a general flavour of the age. And I endeavoured to use as pure Anglo-Saxon as possible in all my conversations." Arthur Conan Doyle.

"A Watsonian Conundrum" just happened one day. I opened the *Watsonian* scholarly journal and in my head, Sherlock Holmes and Doctor Watson were discussing censorship. Then did what Stephen King recommends and wrote it down. [7]

In Doctor Watson's biographical chronicles of Sherlock Holmes, we experience the horror of criminality through the eyes of its victims. Holmes's attention is focused laser-like on his method, while justice or forgiveness comes through the application of his new science. Watson delineates the scene, and we feel like we are there.

> "It is fear, Mr. Holmes. It is terror.' She raised her veil as she spoke, and we could see that she was indeed in a pitiable state of agitation, her face all drawn and grey, with restless, frightened eyes, like those of some hunted

animal. Her features and figure were those of a woman of thirty, but her hair was shot with premature grey, and her expression was weary and haggard." The Adventure of the Speckled Band.

"Miss Annie Harrison's Rose Soliloquy" is a version of Conan Doyle's "The Adventure of the Naval Treaty." In Doyle's story, Miss Harrison is an afterthought. No one introduces her. She doesn't speak during the meeting until after Holmes's ode to a rose. At which point she confronts him. The edicts of society were unbendable during Victorian times. Holmes improvises his rose soliloquy to garner the attention of the only person in the room he could not approach.

Choosing to follow in Doctor Watson's footsteps, most of my stories take place during Victorian or Edwardian times. There is another history I adhere to, the history within the canon of Sherlock Holmes stories. As Watson implies in "A Case of Identity," the mind of Sherlock Holmes can conceive in four dimensions, through generations, and in certain circumstances, through history. Existing many generations away from his day, I time travel whenever I write.

"Life is infinitely stranger than anything which the mind of man could invent... If we could fly out of that window hand in hand, hover over this great city, gently remove the roofs, and peep in at the queer things which are going on, the strange coincidences, the planning's, the cross-purposes, the wonderful chains of events, working through generations, and leading to the most outré results, it would make all fiction with its conventionalities and foreseen conclusions most stale and unprofitable." A Case of Identity.

"Mrs Hudson's Garden" was originally written as the basis of a novel. Nevertheless, Mrs Hudson decided she had much more to say, and the novel transformed into *The Keys of Death*. The garden journal then provided clues to the murderer. This little monograph grew out of my love and experience of gardening plus joyous research into the Arts and Crafts movement of the nineteenth-century.

> "How I loved the small and simple ways of living, the happy absence of all complications, the possibility of living close down to nature that seemed to leave one more freedom to think and to do!" Gertrude Jekyll. [8]

"A Toast Darling" began as a short story, inspired by George Roland Wills's, excellent *A Short Phantasy. Jeremy Brett meets Mr. Sherlock Holmes*. Written four months after Mr Brett's death on Sept. 12, 1995. This tribute moved me to author my story. Yet a portrayal of Jeremy Brett's ebullient joie de vivre could only be shown in a play. [9]

> "I make a point of never having any prejudices and of following docilely wherever fact may lead me." The Adventure of the Reigate Squires.

"A Scandal in Baker Street" expresses some of my research on the subject and a prelude to my novel, *Remarkable Power Of Stimulus*. Here, I look at Holmes's relationship with *the* woman from the point of view of their first meeting. An addition to Doyle's "A Scandal In Bohemia." In my novel, Irene Adler returns to London after nine years away and

Holmes is inexorably drawn to her. Their meeting leads to marriage in an anarchist ridden Paris.

> "I only caught a glimpse of her at the moment, but she was a lovely woman, with a face that a man might die for." A Scandal in Bohemia.

> It was a simple legal ceremony at the 1st Arrondissement office, performed by the mairie – exactly what they required. In minutes they were homme et femme. Mr. and Mrs. Holmes moved onto the terrace, overlooking the Louvre, and the three chromatic scales of the belfry chimed noon. It echoed through the empty plaza as sweet, blossomed trees perfumed the eerily vacant Parisian streets. *Remarkable Power of Stimulus.*

After reading Sir Arthur Conan Doyle's, "The Adventure Of Black Peter," I couldn't get past his ending. What happened to the two sailors waiting in Holmes's bedroom? What did they do there? Doyle hadn't resolved it. Quite possibly one of his many pranks.

The fate of the two seamen stayed with me. This inspiration led to "Black Peter's Misplaced Mariners." To provide a background, I researched the fascinating and horrific history of whaling and then put it in Doctor Watson's capable hands.

> "In dealing with criminal subjects, one's natural endeavour is to keep the crime in the background. In nearly half the number of the Sherlock Holmes stories, however, in a strictly legal sense, no crime was actually

committed at all. One heard a good deal about crime and the criminal, but the reader was completely bluffed. Of course, I could not bluff him always, so sometimes I had to give him a crime, and occasionally I had to make it a downright bad one." Arthur Conan Doyle.[10]

Conan Doyle's relationship with the Sherlock Holmes phenomenon was a stormy one. Though these stories gave him the life he wanted as an author, he was of the opinion that his historical novels deserved more attention. It gladdens me to note that by the end of his life, this was somewhat resolved. Doyle was able to accept the benefits his great detective gave to the world.

"My view has been justified, as I understand that in several countries some change has been made in police procedure on account of these stories. It is all very well to sneer at the paper detective, but a principle is a principle, whether in fiction or in fact. Many of the great lessons of life are to be learned in the pages of the novelist." Sir Arthur Conan Doyle. [11]

Gretchen Altabef
Old Jordan Woods
20 November 2024

Mycroft and Sherlock Holmes [1]

Boxing Day Brother Mine

"I had called upon my friend Sherlock Holmes upon the second morning after Christmas, with the intention of wishing him the compliments of the season. He was lounging upon the sofa in a purple dressing-gown." The Adventure of the Blue Carbuncle.

26 December 1887.

There was no mystery about Sherlock's purple dressing-gown. It was a holiday gift from me, his brother, Mycroft. I thought a little colour added to his limited black-and-white palette might brighten him up a bit.

You probably know that Doctor Watson is the usual teller of these tales, but since this one doesn't concern murder or the good doctor, I take my pen in hand. As in most of Sherlock's life, here too there is a certain degree of danger. Nevertheless, I rarely partake in these puerile adventures, and they are better told by the good doctor.

Oh, yes, Sherlock Holmes has a brother. I am the diplomatic one. I spend my life in stately formal, gold-brocaded Royal sitting rooms. Amid changing political environs, I like to think of myself as my country's second Rock of Gibraltar. But with an Admiral's ability to steer through storms at the elbow of power. This is my milieu, where I shine. Clandestine living becomes me. Like Sherlock, I have created my own profession. I work within the highest levels of the British government, yet no one can pin down exactly what it is I do. Also by design.

Omniscience, though quite normal to my way of thinking, is somewhat rare, yet no one can find fault with my sweeping decisions. My wide-ranging views have gained me a special, if completely confidential, position in Her Majesty's government. One might also say that I am Whitehall's central exchange.

Suppose a minister needs information which involves the Navy, India, Canada, and the bi-metallic question. He could ask for separate advice from various departments upon each. But just imagine how much more efficacious it is to suggest immediately how each factor is affected. That is where I come into it. I can humbly admit that time and again my conclusions have decided the national policy.

My brother Sherlock jokingly refers to me as "The British Government." That may be because of my girth or a desire to cut me down to size. Where he is quick, active, and thin, I am of a more moderate temperament.

Today's 26 December holiday took place in these Isles and colonies immediately after Christmas. Boxing Day or the Feast of Saint Stephen, when even the silent gentlemen of the Diogenes Club must do without. This unique holiday has nothing to do with that great British sport and everything to do with the boxes of gifts that were given to household servants as acknowledgement for their work throughout the year, and was their designated holiday. [2]

On this day, we acknowledged those who, either through choice or misadventure, served us. Secretary, chef, maitre'd, porters, barbers, concierges, tailors, doormen, librarians, wait staff, footmen, laundry, maids, valets, butlers, and those who carried out their requests. Honour gratefully paid to an endless stream of deserving caretakers. [3]

While servants were off celebrating their well-earned holiday, the dearth of their guardianship gave the club a dark and eerie air. The starched brightness of costumes and the deep red velvet of jackets hung ghost-like on hooks. Oriental carpets, members' stuffed high-backed chairs, and even the gold of the stair railing were lacklustre within the shadows of unlit lamps, undrawn window curtains, and cold fireplaces. The day was even more peaceful, for most members had taken refuge elsewhere. [4]

Sherlock referred to the servant-class as the 'London slavey', and organized his life without them. Mrs Hudson managed the house where he lived. She hired a maid to help her with the day-to-day tasks, plus Billy, the boy in buttons, to answer the door and run up to the first-floor with clients or messages, thus saving Mrs Hudson from the constant climb. Then there were the Baker Street Irregulars, the street urchin sleuths whom Sherlock hired as needed. Wiggins, their leader, and Billy were also attending school on Sherlock's dime.

Nevertheless, it was Sherlock's and my tradition to spend Saint Stephen's Day together. The surrounding library quiet of the club was reminiscent of our Yorkshire upbringing, and neither of us had an interest in the derby football matches played on this day. We met in the Stranger's room, the only place in the club that allowed conversation. The rule everywhere else in this singular gentlemen's establishment was that one forfeited their membership after three noisy infractions.

For Sherlock and myself, the deeply shadowed, and empty gentleman's club brought back those rare and mysterious days of our childhood when we were completely unsupervised. At Christmastime, our parents, as squires of the manor, opened their home with elaborate parties and feasts. It was understandable that on Boxing Day, with the servants gone, they would seek each other's quiet company.

Our only job that day was to deliver the family's gift boxes to our neighbours. In return, they plied us with spiked eggnog. Sherlock and I, on this one day a year, probed the old Grange inside and out, to its stables and gardens, in order to discover its cold and lamp-less secrets. We created intellectual scavenger hunts and memory games, which ranged further afield each year. Sherlock usually won these contests.

Through the club's stained-glass library windows stood the great city we had both chosen as adults. My fortunate world existed within the seats of the British government, Whitehall, Windsor, and Buckingham Palace. While Sherlock held a map in his mind of every high or low parish and street on either side of the River Thames. Today, we drank fine wine together and shared a most splendid cold repast with Christmas goose, plum pudding, and other delicacies. What my brother gifted me was a rare Tokay wine. Sherlock never cared for feasts. Food was sustenance and fuel for him. Not so for me. I had a finely cultivated palate. He had excellent taste in wine and other spirits. Our parents raised us as epicures.

When he arrived, I was languishing in velvet and plumped pillows in my finest scarlet smoking jacket. Within the complete silence of an empty club, I was sipping a glass of Veuve Clicquot, 1870, the widow's best, and resting after my preparations. He rushed in dressed in a tattered and rusty black frockcoat and a topper that looked as if a horse had trampled it in the dirt. He entered the little circle of lamplight and candles I had created in the library. We addressed each other properly with a hearty hand clasping.

"My God, Sherlock, come, my barber will despatch that forthwith. Your hair is Jarvey length!"

I rang the bell-pull.

He laughed, "Thank you, but your bell will not bring a barber today, brother mine, and I have not yet completed the task for which it was grown. You must needs accept me as I am. But hurry, Mycroft, the game is afoot!"

He insisted me into my tweed jacket.

"Into your coat and come!"

"Working on a case during the Holidays, I admire your fortitude, little brother."

"A Christmas fancy, brother mine."

"Living undercover in another's shabby suit, Sherlock. If you joined with my Diogenes gentlemen, there would at least be time off."

"Time waits for no gentleman. Mycroft, your laziness is insufferable! Give in, brother, daylight is rather limited today."

"Surely you will share dinner with me, Sherlock?"

He waved it away.

"If you are open to it, I would require your immediate assistance."

As he spoke, he stuffed thick slabs of Christmas goose between two slices of bread, wrapped them in a paper, and with a few strawberry tarts dropped them into his coat pocket.

"Of course," I answered.

"Splendid, I will slip out through the servant's entrance. My horse awaits me there."

"Sherlock, surely this is unnecessary. If you can find an open telegraph office and require my further involvement, send a wire."

"The air of your club is as cold as the icy street! Mycroft, it is crucial that you attend!"

"What have you involved me in?"

"A little Boxing Day cheer," echoed down the stairway with his receding footsteps.

"Complements of the Season, brother mine," I called after him.

He swiftly descended the back stairs and was gone. For a blessed instant, I considered the serene day rolling out ahead of me. Then downed my champagne, moved the feast into the icebox, speedily donned coat, hat, and gloves and escaped into the December chill through the entrance for club members. When I joined Sherlock minutes later in his cab, he was all business and sporting an East End accent.

"Oy, where to, luv?" he showed his perfect set of teeth, the only giveaway to his costume.

With the agility of a youth, he leapt up to his seat and started the horse.

"You have chosen wisely. Ole Jack knows the city like the back of 'is hand! Please kindly honour Saint Stephen's Day before you leave me, sir."

He touched his hat.

My brother's sense of humour was never a favourite of mine. Yet, in a trice, we had surfaced in Pall Mall and pointed towards Bloomsbury at a swift pace. I was aware Sherlock's plans would reveal themselves in good time and happy that between the university and the museum; he had chosen a respectable neighbourhood for his holiday fancy.

We slowly paced Tottenham Court Road to the back and halted at a lonely Inn.

"This will do," my brother said as he drew the reins and applied the brake.

Sherlock hopped down, petted the horse affectionately, and handed the reins to a dirty street urchin. He then dropped the sandwich into the boy's right pocket and the tarts into his left and patted his head.

He quickly scanned my attire and pried from me my stick, hat, and coat, leaving these supreme symbols of a gentleman's attire in the carriage.

In character, he said to me, "Thank ye for yer generosity, guv."

I laughed, "If all else fails, you still have a Jarvey's occupation to fall back on, Sherlock."

He drew me close, "Keep alert, Mycroft, this is no folly! The life of an innocent man threatened with seven years of hard labour is at stake. This Public House is not Pall Mall nor the Diogenes' Club. Your highborn friends will not help you here."

Sherlock threw the least offensive of the carriage rugs over my shoulders, pinned it with a tarnished rose broach, and crowned me with what looked like one of Doctor Watson's old, discarded caps. Then he put his arm through mine, and we entered the Old Alpha Inn as extremely disreputable brothers together.

It was indeed a lively place, filled with celebration and holiday cheer. Sherlock relit his soggy cigar and tipped his hat to the landlord. The Pub was gas and candlelit, festive Christmas Holly adorned every fireplace and doorway. Wooden tables with full groaning benches kept grateful men warming at the blazing hearths. It was clear from the expectancy and enthusiasm shown by their audience that the final darts tournament of the year was underway. It was lit by additional candelabra and boisterous with loud concomitant wagering. Sherlock talked for a moment with the landlord. Then he led me to a nearby table and brought over two pints.

"What is this, Sherlock?"

I pulled out my red silk handkerchief to dust off the bench. But my brother instantly thrust it back into my breast pocket with a growl and a look of fire in his eyes.

"Sit down and be patient, my dear Mycroft! And leave your snuff box in your pocket," he hissed.

"Sherlock, what does this have to do with me?"

"Yesterday, brother mine, Commissionaire Peterson, shared with me his Christmas Eve mystery. He observed a man carrying a splendid white goose over his shoulder who was put upon by roughs in this neighbourhood. In the scuffle, he lost his hat, and his Christmas goose, and accidentally shattered the window of a local establishment when he raised his stick in self-defence. Peterson rushed to protect the man from his assailants, but they all took to their heels. The Commissionaire retrieved the battered hat and goose and brought them to me to solve the dilemma.

"'For Mrs Henry Baker' was printed on a small card tied to the bird's left leg, and the initials 'H. B.' were legible upon the lining of the hat. These were my only clues; but, as there are some thousands of Bakers and some hundreds of Henry Bakers in this city of ours, it is not a simple thing to restore lost property to any one of them." [5]

"Sherlock, my mind is just as full of essential facts as is yours, yet I have not memorised the London telephone book!"

"Nor would it help you here, brother mine. It was only right that the goose would go to Peterson's family dinner, while I retained Henry Baker's hat."

"I will never understand your love of trifles. Where does this lead us?"

"Today, we shall scour these Public Houses in search of the roughs who attacked Mr Baker."

"Who may be a tough on Christmas Eve, may be a family man on Christmas Day, eh, Sherlock?"

"Exactly. The holiday changes everything. And I would rather be led to the scene of the crime by one who was there than search through every street for the right shop."

"I celebrate your choice of a warm inn. Sherlock, is this why we are here in this establishment instead of surrounded by the comforts of my club?"

"It is the game, Mycroft! Your Diogenes Club is cold and deserted. It is highly probable that Watson is soaking in the Northumberland Street Baths after his Old-Timers football match. However, our game is of paramount importance as John Horner must be got off." [6]

"I read in *The Times* he was arrested for stealing the Blue Carbuncle. They accuse him of a previous charge for theft, Sherlock. But why be concerned with such an artless case?"

"The man is innocent, Mycroft! Yet what Scotland Yard inspector will probe the clues to demonstrate it? It is a second conviction to them. You are free of your customary duties, as am I. Since we unite today as family, brother, I thought you might indulge me in the solving of this remarkable little mystery."

"I am Watson in this scenario?"

"No, no, no, Mycroft, you are my elder brother, with a brain of greater capacity than mine. And I thought you might enjoy a taste of how lives the common man. Rejoice in your pint, brother. The landlord confided to me their ale has a reputation for rich, wine-like flavour, and strength. Further that Henry Baker was one of a knot of regulars who lounged in the warmth of the British Museum during the day. This sojourn may soon be concluded."

Sherlock has always been interested in the other classes. He believed in the equality of all. He partnered with a fine middle-class gentleman, a soldier, and a doctor. However, I find Mrs Hudson's crowded upper floor to be quite beneath a Holmes! We have descended from Squires, so we are gentlemen, nonetheless! While I couldn't do my work without this distinction. He frequently found it a barrier to his.

"Mycroft, keep an eye on that darts player, a violent man," my brother whispered.

Sherlock was up in a flash. He took the next turn at darts and threw four bullseyes for the team, which was glad to have him. But the man he had indicated was not. That he had a violent nature was apparent in his surly demeanour. He had the stamp of every school bully upon him, though I doubt he ever attended much school.

"Who the hell are you?"

"I'm fillin' in!"

"A ratbag ringer, that's wot!"

"Fair 'n square!"

"Not in my book! Get out of it!"

While Sherlock assessed his man, shouts and threats filled my end of the pub. Another row was developing right in front of me. It centred around a friend I had recognised, the butler from the Tankerville Club, who was discreetly drinking across from me. An observant rough realised the man was celebrating the Boxing Day Holiday and taunted him.

"Who the bloody dickens do you think you are? What makes you so different that you deserve a special holiday and Christmas boxes?"

He pushed the butler.

"I work like you do. Where's my holiday? Where's my drafted boxes?"

"No different from you, sir. I am here, as you are, hiding from my good woman on a day of rest."

"Now, 'es telling me fortune! Shut your saucebox and share those gifts! Come on, give us a wee peek."

He laughed loudly and elbowed the butler hard. I had to step in to defend the man.

I addressed him cordially, "My good man, you are mistaken. There is no cause for derision. This man's job is to superbly care for a full club of gentlemen and very much deserves his day off."

I patted the first man's back in a friendly way. He moved away from my hand as if it were on fire. Then he turned to me and knocked off my cap.

"Who're you? I wasn't talking to you, Mr Jollocks! You sound like you know this mumbling cove and maybe belong to his almighty club. What's a gentleman doing here in our pub? Or is Mr High and Mighty spying on us? Admit it, gents, don't 'e look like a spy?"

Sherlock pushed his way through the laughing, jeering crowd that had formed around the butler and me. He stood next to me in a fighter's stance.

"Gentlemen, surely this difference of opinion is not worth a rumbumptious anointing? What will your Misses say to a blooded nose or even a half-mourning blinker?"

"From you? You're as skinny as Job's turkey. Better watch that parish pick-axe don't weigh you down. You're off your chump!"

I watched incredulously as the foolish man actually took a swing at Sherlock. I had no fear, for my brother was a semi-pro, bare-knuckled boxer. He acquired his pugilist skill first at Cambridge and then in the private clubs, boxing in the ring with those who were far superior to his ability. Yet once he learned the sport, no one could beat him, for my brother's other talents assisted him in predicting his opponent's next move.

I was enjoying this outing and joined in the betting that had instantly encircled the two men.

"To the blood, brother mine," I yelled above the betting.

Sherlock smiled and parried the man's thrown punch, stopping his arm in mid-flight. Then he knocked him down with three rapid-fire lefts to the jaw. From behind, the darts chucker joined in the fray. Sherlock shifted, then addressed the man's wrist with baritsu forcing him to his knees and then the floor. When he again gained his feet, my brother threw his signature uppercut. Both men went down. We escorted the butler and the two scoundrels outside for questioning. As soon as we gained the pavement, we sent the butler on his way home.

"I don't know no bloody Henry Baker!" the man who began the altercation said, blood streaming from his nose dotted the snow.

My brother gave him a handkerchief.

Sherlock said, "Late Christmas Eve, you were part of a group of toughs who tormented Mr Baker, instead of wishing him the complements of the season. A commissionaire approached you and you all ran, leaving behind Baker's sizable Christmas goose and his old bowler hat."

"So what if we did? You're no bloody mutton-shunter."

He extended his hand. "My name is Sherlock Holmes and I am looking for Mr Baker. If you can direct me to the shop with the broken window, I'll give each of you a half-sovereign."

This changed the energy completely. The air of danger receded and its opposite expressed itself.

"I'm Barney. And would you, sir, be Doctor Watson?"

Sherlock answered, "Forgive me. This is my friend, Mike."

I smiled and tipped my cap. Barney put out his hand. Sherlock elbowed me into action, and I shook the man's hand. His grip was surprisingly commanding, reminiscent of Sir James Walter of the Admiralty.

The darts man introduced himself as Tommy. Throughout, he hurried Barney along with cold-related comments, and the men quickly brought us to the Goodge Street crime scene.

"He broke the window of that wine shop." Tommy pointed at the debris. "I'll bet his stick is still there, gov! But none of us knew him."

Sherlock gave each a half-sovereign and released them. I watched as they stomped their way through the snow and headed back towards the Alpha. My brother was analysing the scene before us. He paced with light, swift steps about the area. I felt it was obsessive, especially in the cold weather, yet he called out important points to me.

"Stay where you are, Mycroft! Though damaged easily, snow is the best substance for foot impresses. The scuffle took place here. Mycroft, can you see where these footprints overlap in the snow? Here's the commissionaire running tiptoes on top of them! Baker's stick went through the shop window. Recently smashed. It is gone. A shame. I had hoped it would have led me to him."

"Sherlock, are you satisfied? I'm freezing!"

He paid the street urchin who immediately ran inside the warm Public House. We mounted the carriage. Sherlock in his cabbie persona drove me back to the Diogenes Club, where he took the rug from me and swaddled the horse in its warmth.

As the short winter sun coloured the Stranger's Room windows, I added coal and wood to the fire and handed my brother a warming brandy. Then brought out our cold repast. We pulled chairs up to the blazing fire and talked over the day. Sherlock threw his cigar into the flames, downed his drink, and sat rubbing his hands together for warmth.

"Sherlock, you see importance where no one else can. It was exhilarating, but what was that about?"

"You know my methods, Mycroft."

"Not as well as you do. For instance, how did you single out your suspect? To me, he was the same as all the others."

"That is your blindness. I make a point of never having any prejudices and of following docilely wherever fact may lead me. The man was wearing a scarf of green and gold Baker Clan plaid knotted around his neck. A simple thing."

"Ah, ha! He may be related to Baker, or he stole the scarf. Either way, you win, Sherlock."

"Yes, and the fact that as soon as he realised my purpose, he hid this adornment deep inside his coat underlined my deductions. But Mycroft, surely you noticed this."

"What I observed was the fact that the shop window had a circular break at the point of impact. Broken glass radiated out from that central point, so Baker's cane must have a metal top to match it."

"That is a fine observation for a scavenger hunt. Yet, in deduction, it is necessary to sift through clues and keep only the relevant ones. Speculations without facts to back them up can lead to an exhaustive pursuit of an erroneous scent. Are they your only conclusions from this year's Boxing Day games, brother?"

"Of course not, most the patrons of the Alpha Inn were humorously enjoying each other's company, while one or two were agitators. I find this same state of affairs can exist in any group of people, even in political meetings where the agitators might serve a purpose. Maybe I ought to offer half sovereigns the next time I encounter such? Then there was the fact that you brought me into a dangerous situation, brother. Now, please enjoy some of this splendid goose, dear boy. Where will you go from here?"

Sherlock sighed, "I must return the horse and then will await further developments. Mycroft, you know John Horner has already spent his holiday's in the cold cells of Pentonville Prison."

I thought it the right moment to gift him his pub winnings, which he accepted with a laugh.

"Thank you, gov!" he said.

We finished the wine, and I succeeded in serving him the goose, pudding, mince pie, and the rest.

Following our feast, I poured out two tumblers full of brandy and handed one to my brother. He nodded his thanks and accepted a cigar. I was not a pipe fancier. I preferred the refinement and violet perfume of royal snuff. But Sherlock revelled in his smoke.

"I wonder if Mr Baker might not give it up as a loss and just purchase a new hat, Sherlock?"

"Quite possibly, Mycroft, yet just as possible is that the story will continue when I advertise the found goose and hat, which will bring him to Baker Street at 6:30 o'clock tomorrow."

I fed the fire once again. We watched as the flames flashed and flared, throwing animated shadows on the stone walls of the large hearth.

"What did you think of my Boxing Day game, Mycroft?"

"Somewhat reminiscent of the year the Vicar caught us after one too many eggnogs and the carols that were enriched by our unforgettable harmonising."

Sherlock laughed, "Yes, that also was an excellent Boxing Day diversion, brother mine."

We then toasted the day, and those who served us, our brotherhood, our friends, and the coming New Year 1888.

Mycroft Holmes
The Diogenes Club
26 December 1887

Note: Boxing Day commences the day before Doctor Watson's original story. To discover what occurs during the next three days, and the conclusion to this adventure. I highly recommend reading one of the good doctor's best, "The Adventure of the Blue Carbuncle."

Albert Robida "The Future Imagined" La vie électrique. [1]

Sir Arthur & The Time Machine

Awarded the ACD Society's Doylean Honours for Fiction.

It was one of those rare experiences which can be looked upon as educational. At the time, it seemed to be leading to my very downfall. Now, with time behind me, I can acknowledge that I gained—well, as I tell you the story, you will learn what I gained. You may believe me or not, but it was one of the most transformative episodes of my adventurous life.

Overnight, an unpredictably loud and demanding thunder and lightning storm visited our South London home. Yet no rain to wash away the peasouper that hugged the foundations and hung over rooftops. I awoke from a nightmare with no recuperative sleep. The change in atmosphere affected my poor wife, and her coughing began in earnest, bringing the horror of my dream into reality. It was an all too familiar turn of events in our lives lately. I held her hand for a moment and then went to my bag to administer a calmative. She was not getting better. We had recently returned to attend the Fortescue Award Dinner, where I was the principal speaker. My life was in London, yet her tuberculin scarred lungs needed the rarefied air of Alpine Switzerland.

I could wait no longer. This was the only solution that held hope. I called in a nurse to stay with my wife and travelled by horse-drawn cab the eleven miles from South Norwood to Richmond. My particular friend H. G. Wells was one of the best men of his day at everything connected with time or the fourth dimension. He had spoken largely upon the subject, had travelled to places no modern man will again, and finally, he had created a considerable sensation with his Time Machine.

My solution was here. It had to be. Though I was doing my damnedest, I was failing. And I had begun to worry for my sanity. It was necessary that I discuss my thoughts with Wells. Undoubtedly, he would hear me and see my need. I was nervous and jittery, and the least word disturbed me, especially anything about Holmes.

I sent him crashing to the bottom of the Reichenbach Fall. Why was he still haunting me?

But this was not like me. I took things in hand. Freud had no answers except hypnosis, and I was not a suitable subject. A cure for tuberculosis and psychology are infants today. If I could move ahead and witness them further along, why should not exceptional answers appear?

Wells and I gathered in his comfortable drawing-room. The very room he first unveiled his thoughts about the nature of time. The fireplace was gently flashing, candles were lit, surrounded by the comfort of oak wood panelling and deep red Persian rugs, plus the perfume of gentlemanly tobacco greeted one. We had progressed from dinner to brandy and discussion.

"Arthur, I was sorry to hear about the loss of your beloved father. Such a shame."

I bowed my head.

"Thank you."

I stepped to the humidor and lit a cigar. A servant handed me a brandy snifter and left us alone. My pacing stopped, and I stood at the fire.

"Wells, we've been friends for years. And I have always kept silent in deference to your reticence about this topic, especially since your run-in with the scientific press. Your papers and stories about time travel have always intrigued me,

— but circumstances in my life force me to these questions. Is it possible for a 19th-Century scientist to travel ahead in time to specific dates and people—and return intact?"

"Doyle, whenever we hold a memory in our consciousness, we are essentially travelling in time."

He gestured to me.

"But are you all right? I can see you are highly agitated, not at all your usual mirthful self. I fear for you, my friend. What major storm has flooded your life, Doctor?" he said.

"I have not been myself since my father's death—"

He led me to a comfortable chair, and we sat on either side of the fire.

"And killing off that damned Holmes! I was overjoyed to be rid of him. Yet, twenty thousand readers cancelled their subscriptions to *The Strand Magazine* in protest. Twenty thousand! It is clear that my fans have chosen him over me."

"How is your family?"

"They are well. No, no, that will not do. My wife has been diagnosed with incurable Tuberculosis—"

Wells reached out and put his hand on my forearm.

"Oh, Doyle, I am so sorry."

"I am frantically researching the disease, but present-day knowledge is paltry. She will spend much of the rest of her brief life in Swiss Spas. Yet I believe the future holds tremendous promise."

Wells started from his chair.

"There are great liabilities as well as great benefits to time travel."

Of course, I knew of the loss of his scientific standing over the previous unveiling of his Time Machine. He knew my integrity and friendship would never bring a similar result.

Nevertheless, what I had in mind was a more directed use of his machine, and I turned towards him.

"But do you have it, man?"

"Come with me, Doyle."

He ushered me to a securely locked circular solarium at the back of his house. At one time, his laboratory opened into the superbly tended garden. Ivy had been allowed to grow over the windows, and little light appeared to help our way. He opened the door and turned up the lamps. Their brightness after the dark hall reflected wildly on the polished and dazzling crystalline and golden brass object sitting in the middle of his laboratory.

I ran to it and then grabbed the lapels of my friend's rather unusual jacket like a desperate man. I could see he was scrutinising me, my sanity, considering my pleas and the future of his time machine.

"Does it work? Can you tell it where to go? Can you come back? How is it fuelled? When can I travel in it? Will you come with me? Will it age me to do so?"

I dropped his coat in embarrassment.

"Doyle, the answer to all except fuel and myself is 'Yes.' It's fuelled electrically by a holding battery to start and then needs nothing. But you must recharge it electrically for your return. And that is easier to achieve in the future. Also, much training in how it works is necessary. I would hate to lose you and my marvellous machine."

"It ages you?"

Wells sat on a divan and pointed to a chair. I could not sit.

"That is the sole reason it is situated here in the dust. As far as I am able to calculate, one minute there is equivalent to one day here. You must watch your time. I lost thirty years of my life in its active research, forfeited friends and family, returned to a tumbledown home and ruin as a scientist. But knowing what I know now, I would abandon my studies, anyway."

He put his hand on my shoulder.

"Yet, as you know, my career as a writer has flourished. Doyle, time is only another kind of space. When I speak of time, I am talking about a physical plane, a material dimension like length, breadth, and height. We believe we travel in one direction along a vast measurement from the starting point to the ending point of our lives. But I have found it is possible to break through reality's rules and produce slight fissures in the space of time."

I paced the room.

"Whatever the cost, I must leave here for a time and find answers in the future!"

"I'm afraid that some of that cost, my dear Arthur, maybe your belief in science, and would not advise travel to times adjacent to ours. If you should happen upon your own future achievements, steer clear. The knowledge would be too personal to bear."

I grabbed his hand and shook it heartily to seal our bargain.

He agreed to allow me into his experiment and instructed me to keep a scientific journal. In ten days of intense study, Wells taught me how to care for the Time Machine. He also installed a Cosmic Density Irregulator device, which he said would make things easier.

"Doyle, it is possible to utilise the natural intervals in the fourth dimension. Like a crystal ball reflecting through the universe, a portal appears almost as simply as opening a three-dimensional doorway. My Time Machine creates the opening, where and when it occurs, is a matter of how one sets the Transversable Achronal Gauges and the Retrograde Domain Indicators."

His tutoring was excellent. Knowing all its intricacies only intensified my awe at his creation. My knowledge was complete on every point before he would permit me to take her out. After a good night's sleep and a hearty breakfast, we readied for this new exploration. Wells took my vitals and wrote them down, along with the date and time.

I, Arthur Ignatius Conan Doyle, M.D. advanced to the Time Machine. Dressed as Wells advised me, in my most modern short coat, boots, tie and cap, with essentials to be pawned in my pockets. My mind was racing with anticipation. My thoughts were full of the thrill of the unknown. Plus the fear of everything I knew and what could go wrong.

Was this experiment my elaborate undoing? Would I wind up a maniac lost somewhere in time? Was this how Arthur Conan Doyle would end, with the death of Holmes as my final story and an unfulfilled speaking tour of America?

As Wells had instructed me, I operated the controls and arrived instantaneously in New York City at 10:50 pm, 9 December 1980. I pushed the new Cosmic Density Irregulator button and in a flash, the time machine devolved neatly into a briefcase. Assaulted by the noise, overwhelmed by sounds I had never heard screeching around me, fast transport, and buildings that blotted out the sky. My rugger goalie reflexes kept me from being run down by a police car, its siren and lights blazing as it hurtled into the emergency entrance of Roosevelt Hospital behind me. Its 19th-Century red-brick façade was a most welcome sight. I followed in as a doctor in a hospital was a better place for me to acclimate to 1980. Lights were flashing around us in the tunnel when I reached the motorcar as the body was lifted onto a cart and rushed into the hospital. By the amount of blood, I doubted the man on the stretcher had long to live. The officers pushed their way in through the entrance.

"Take him to the Operating Theatre immediately!" I said.

Rushing in after them, I was astonished by the amount of suffering around me. Addicts and alcoholics screaming in withdrawal, wounded, children in pain and fever, aged praying for help, street beggars, their dirt-darkened skin peeling, Mycobacterium lepromatosis. My training at Edinburgh Hospital never readied me for this. They looked like war wounded, only there was no war.

I donned the white coat of my profession and ran down the corridor. In the wake of the cart, hospital staff grabbed telephones or began crying together. I followed the trail of blood leading to the Emergency Operating Room, where I secured my briefcase in a locker. The signs above the scrubs cubbies made it clear. I donned the strange blue material over my hair and shoes. Masked, I scrubbed and stretched on amazingly skin-tight gloves.

I instructed the police officers to alert the hospital of their arrival and entered the operating theatre. Stepped up to the table and assessed the man's wounds. I reached for his pulse, looked into his eyes, observed his colour, and knew. Then I diagnosed the cause of death. The wounds resulted from pistol shots at close range. Two bullets discharged in the posterior aspect of the trunk, two to the left portion of the shoulder and the left anterior wall of the chest. All had exit wounds. There was damage to his left lung, the left subclavian artery, and, severely, to his heart. It was evident he had lost an enormous amount of blood. He looked English, and it was fitting I thought that an attending doctor at the end of his life was Scottish. I took the man's hand in mine.

"Another journey awaits you, young man. Go with our blessings."

As it was now beyond my skill, I closed his eyes and added my notes to his chart. Then deposited my used scrubs in the bin with the big sign and retraced my steps through the halls. A surgical team of seven ran swiftly by me.

All along the pathway, I witnessed nurses and staff crying yet bravely resuming their positions. A song began playing over the hospital announcement system. I queried a nurse, who was deeply affected.

"Don't you recognise it? *All My Lovin* is a Beatles song."

She wiped her eyes and continued.

"The man who died here just minutes ago was the great John Lennon. I can't believe it. I thought he'd live forever."

She burst into tears. I patted her hand and handed her my handkerchief.

Then I passed from the hallway to the main entrance. Posted there was unlooked-for assistance for my quest, a small sign, Octavo-sized, bulletined with many others. Why I picked it out of the morass was due to my teacher, Doctor Bell. His constant insistence that observation was a doctor's most important tool.

Smither's Building:
Hope for the Children of Alcoholics
Wednesday, 8 pm
Alcoholics Anonymous
Tues., Thurs., Sun., 8 pm

I thought, *Hope for the Children of Alcoholics? Too late in the day for children—are these things so out in the open in the future? Promising research begins tonight!* I took my pencil and a small journal from my waistcoat pocket and jotted down the particulars. The Smithers Building was just next door. Then I went looking for a newspaper and somewhere to pawn one of the items Wells had pressed upon me.

An hour later, I sat in Ray's Pizzeria on Upper Broadway, munching my first slice of New York Pizza and drinking greasy coffee, engrossed in the *New York Times*. I queried the owner for a good barber. He directed me to the Hotel Beacon, which was my predetermined destination. Under strict orders from Wells, I disguised myself. In the barber chair, my hair was lightened, and cut to the style of the day, and my moustache eliminated. We discussed beards, and I found myself unsuited for a goatee.

Clean-shaven for the first time since boyhood, I checked in and was established comfortably in a suite at the four-star hotel on Broadway at 65th Street.

Before dinner, I cabbed across town to Bloomingdales in search of up-to-date clothes. At first, it was overwhelming, as if twenty Liberty's Emporiums were packed on top of each other and built of shiny chrome. I wondered how anyone could find their way. A lovely young sales lady took me in hand.

In menswear, I was attended by a gentleman who could have fit just as well in Victorian times. It was disappointing there was no good English tweed to be had, nor any waistcoats. *Where do they keep their watches or pocketbooks?* Watson would be completely flummoxed as to how to carry his service revolver. Still, the lightweight wool suits were extremely comfortable.

From within the changing closet, I said.

"Is this all you wear, even in winter? They are so light. You are not joking, just this? I'll be damned!"

The store sent my new suits plus every colour of men's briefs along to the Hotel Beacon.

I purchased a quick meal from a hotdog vendor on the east side of Central Park and ate my dinner, walking across Fifty-ninth Street, traversing the park's southern end to Roosevelt Hospital. Nothing like a Fortnum & Mason hamper, yet I had been told it was distinctly New York. Inside the Smithers Building was a large room filled with folding chairs. A wall of windows overlooked the lights of the west side and the red glow of the receding sun dappled the ever-changing surface of the Hudson River.

With a genial handshake, I was welcomed into an 'AA' meeting. This meeting was full of gallows humour. Men and women guffawed at the mention of most dire circumstances because the situation was something they shared. I thought, *My father would have loved this camaraderie.*

Later in my rooms, from the founder's books, I discovered this wholly independent organisation began with an Alcoholic Doctor and an Alcoholic Stock Broker. Both were diagnosed as incurable. Together in 1935, they formed this alliance and invited others into it. They believed they could win over this horrible malady in fellowship, that each man or lady who stayed sober strengthened all of them.

The following day, during a superb breakfast in the Amsterdam Room, I questioned the staff about nearby libraries. The morning edition of every newspaper had large headlines and photographs of the gentleman I attended yesterday. He was important to many people, especially to

England. I was grateful to have been able to give such service. This part of Manhattan was thronged with thousands of young people singing his songs and creating memorials. Central Park had become their site of mourning. It was a touching scene.

I walked down Broadway to spend my day in the Lincoln Center Library researching future time trips and the men who could offer the most assistance to me. New York had conveniently numbered streets, which made it simple to traverse. In the evening, I strode south to the theatre district.

The literary scene of the day was both colourful and disturbing. Broadway's great white way seemed to have been captured by the music halls. But I saw enough to know Wilde would love it. He was much-trumpeted here. A great liberation has occurred among his people, extravagant revelries commence each year to celebrate, and he would especially love that. If it were possible to spirit Oscar away from the West End, he would be very much at home in present-day New York.

Back in my hotel rooms, the porter, Mr. Smith, delivered the Bloomies bags and turned on my 'TV'. He hung my suits and instructed me on the machine's adjustments. I turned off the sound. But the image I saw was Sherlock Holmes. I was both transfixed and enraged.

"The world's most famous detective, Sherlock Holmes: Starring Geoffrey Whitehead, Donald Pickering, and Patrick Newell." [2]

Each episode was a separate entity, revealing another crime where Holmes quickly and reliably solved the riddle and saved his client from harm.

"He's wearing an Inverness Cape and a deerstalker like Doctor Bell! In London, preposterous, he'd be laughed out of town."

I thought, *What is this, 'the world's most famous detective?' You bastard, how did you manage this without me? Obviously, you have haunted others, you fiend! 'Based on the characters created by Sir Arthur Conan Doyle.' What does that mean? I killed him in 1893! They cut my characters out of my stories and wrote fresh stories for them; it seems they borrowed an idea or two. Holmes somehow survived and used the fall to separate from me! The hound, is it possible to sue the future?* "Sir?"

Mr. Smith was witness to my ravings, but spoke calmly.

"Doctor Doyle, there is a bookshop I recommend you visit and a fine walk from here. It might widen your perspective."

The evening was still bright and brisk as I walked to Fifty-Sixth Street and travelled east past Seventh Avenue to the Mysterious Bookshop. [3] Entering in, I looked up my books and instantly discovered why Smith recommended this visit.

Encompassing an entire wall in the central part of the store were floor-to-ceiling bookcases filled with my adventures. Much more than I have written. Also, something entitled "Sherlock Holmes Pastiche." No other author or character had that distinction here, a heady realisation. But I remembered Wells's warning, and did not purchase any of my future books, only offerings from the pastiche section.

I cornered Mr. Penzler. [4]

"How did all this happen?"

I rattled off some of the names before me.

"Carr, Rosenberg, Stout, Starrett, Queen, Sayers, and other Sherlock Holmes authors on your shelves—surely, the originals by A. Conan Doyle were enough?"

Penzler studied me for a moment.

"Where have you been?"

I shifted my weight to the other foot and tweaked my non-existent moustache, wondering if I had been found out.

He continued.

"Well, not everyone is aware of what goes on in the literary world. But everyone knows Sherlock Holmes! Many people believe he actually lived. No. 221B, Baker Street is the most famous address in the world."

"People think he lived—Ridiculous!"

"That might be, but there are hundreds of Sherlockian and Holmesian literary societies throughout the world filled with perfectly sane and respectable people who believe both Holmes and Watson lived and are alive today. Since 1911, they have been studying and commenting on those sixty stories, beginning with Oxford's Monsignor Ronald A. Knox."

"That fool!"

"Possibly, but Sir Arthur Conan Doyle created the most enduring character of all times in Holmes. And the pairing with Doctor Watson was genius."

"Thank you," I said, "Ah, for your time, Mr. Penzler."

Did he say "Sir?"

I shook his hand and moved to leave before I gave myself away further.

"Nice meeting you, sir, but you have the advantage of me," he said.

"Vernet."

I waved my way out the door. Hefted my bags of books and stepped into a cab for the ride uptown. Laughing, I was extremely happy that I had followed Wells's directions for discrete costuming. Yet there were times my humour got the better of me.

At 7:45 pm, I walked down Broadway to discover Hope for the Children of Alcoholics. Gallows humour was liberally mixed with tears of grief and awakening. Like AA, there was an understanding that the pure light of truth was spoken here. I had never experienced anything like it. Emancipation waited beneath the lies and secrets of living in an alcoholic home. A young gentleman, the same age as my brother, Innis, related the story of how he grew up. He told of his violent beatings. What I felt was jaw-dropping. It was the story of life with my father.

That young gentleman's story was the key that unlocked my own past. At first, it was overwhelming. I could not control the rage that consumed me or stop sobbing. I could not think or sleep. This was grief, deep intense grief that came up from my very being. I have always had command of myself, thought this was bravery, and that a stiff upper lip defined a man. I had no idea the fire that burnt through my writing could also burn me.

Returning to Wells, we discussed whether I should continue. I was adamant that this must be followed to its conclusion. Later, we shared time stories as we prepared his machine.

He laughed.

"Doyle, in my travels, I did not always wind up where I wanted to be. The time was perfect, but not always the place. I was lucky I didn't land inside a three-dimensional solid."

Wells again took my vitals and jotted them with the date and time in his journal.

My second time trip was fearless and brought me to 1936 and Doctor Albert Einstein. Princeton University's Institute for Advanced Study is in the State of New Jersey. I dropped my alias with him—if anyone could appreciate time travel, it would be he. He understood the design and mechanism of Well's Time Machine at once. Doctor Einstein looked as delighted as a child with a new toy. Excitedly, he went over it from stem to stern. That the construction of this unparalleled vehicle was achieved through 19th-Century materials was a source of Doctor Einstein's delight.

As I watched his intellectual elation, I found it difficult to comprehend that this exceptional man had been persecuted as a Jewish gentleman in his home country and a pacifist in his chosen one. Albert Einstein's remarkable mind brought him to realms far advanced of his day. He also possessed the rare and exquisite ability to teach and communicate what he found there. We shared similar views, although his were more open than mine or anyone's. He understood aspects of the world that I could never entertain. The invisible was made visible through his exceptional mind. Of course, I was a man of the 19th-Century, and he was the 20th-Century. The Professor's mind was more diverse and welcoming than any man I had met.

He invited me to share one of his favourite activities. We took his sailboat up Carnegie Lake in and out of the practising crews. Master of his craft, he caught the wind and skilfully drove our sail while it blew his hair perilously around, and he stuffed it underneath a cap.

With the boom on the starboard side and his hand on the tiller, he was free to question me.

"*Warum?* Why did you kill Sherlock Holmes, Sir Arthur?"

I attempted to change the subject.

"This country is filled with such beauty. Thank you for sharing it with me."

Undaunted in the least, he warned me we would be jibing, and I ducked the boom as it passed over me. Professor Einstein moved his craft to the lake's centre, where the wind was now at our backs.

He smiled at me.

"Sir Arthur, my most challenging ideas arise or are solved in this activity."

Einstein persisted.

"You staged the battle of two brilliant men. Their first meeting was powerfully conceived. Not so their conclusion."

"Everyone is a critic," I laughed.

"But Sir Arthur, don't you see? Your Sherlock Holmes represents genius to the world."

He included me in this.

"And in a world of Lestrade's and Gregson's, we need compelling representation."

He steered past a crew. They raised their oars in salute, and Professor Einstein laughed and waved back.

I shifted our conversation to the pacifism he was devoted to and his hope for the establishment of a World Government. How this would abolish the need for war as an impossible way to solve problems. I shared with him my hope for the reunification of Britain and America, expressing the idea that this could go a long way toward establishing that World

Government. He shook his head at me. And I knew there was a history he had experienced that was still ahead of me.

Einstein's genius was at once powerful and human. Mesmerising in the way talent recognised genius and could get lost in its study. Yet, he was approachable and so human. His students were remarkably fortunate. If my time were not so limited, this was where I would choose to remain.

After much-needed New Jersey embrocation, Professor Einstein and I fired up Well's Time Machine, and I sailed on to December 1980. His cheery, *"Auf Wiedersehen!"* rang in my ears.

For time trip three, my ensuing destination was sunny and warm California, to attend the play, *The Crucifer of Blood*, at the Ahmanson Theatre in Los Angeles. [5] It starred Charlton Heston as Sherlock Holmes and Jeremy Brett as Doctor Watson. That night, the curtain came down on a play that was an insult to me and one of my most acclaimed novels. Heston was unavailable, but Brett welcomed me backstage.

Mr Brett was an exceedingly handsome man. Over six feet tall, with an exquisite British temperament, an immense joie de vie, and an uncharacteristically deep California tan. His powerful voice reminded me of Sir Henry Irving.

I strode into his dressing room and greeted him.

"This play is a bastardisation of Arthur Conan Doyle's novel *The Sign of Four*!"

Brett smiled and invited me to join him while he removed his stage make-up.

"Yes, I am aware of that, but don't you think it's important to bring Doyle's story into the present? Won't it inspire the audience to take down that dusty book and read it again?"

He smoked and sat his cigarette in an ashtray. Then gestured to a bottle of champagne for me to open while he towelled the cold cream from his face. I poured two glasses.

"An intelligent answer," I said.

Mr Brett stood and raised his glass to me.

"To the greatest friendship of all time, our darling Mr Holmes and Doctor Watson."

I touched my glass to his.

"And to the author, Arthur Conan Doyle."

"Hear, hear!" he said and refilled our glasses.

I said, "The stories should be read, of course, produced for the stage and on film. Surely the originals, the author's own words which have stood the test of time, would be better than this imaginative travesty."

"That is an idea."

He sat cross-legged in his chair and paused in his towelling to send a plume of smoke above us.

"Tell me, why is your co-star playing Sherlock Holmes so stiff? He is unreal, galumphing around the stage. And he doesn't speak English! There is no elegance in the man. Holmes is conceited and spoiled, but he is also brilliant, a genius with lightning deductive reasoning. He is a master of sword, stick, British boxing, and baritsu. He moves with the grace of a cat. This actor shows him an ignorant, brutish bore. Your roles should be reversed."

Mr Brett laughed and crushed out his cigarette.

"I am glad my dear friend Charlton isn't here. You don't write for the *L.A. Times* or the *San Francisco Examiner,* do you?"

"No, definitely not!"

"Then are you a member of the Sherlock Holmes Society or The Baker Street Irregulars?"

I guffawed.

"They call themselves The Baker Street Irregulars?"

I laughed again.

"Who are they?"

"One of the oldest Sherlock Holmes literary societies in the world."

I calmed myself to pay him a compliment.

"Mr Brett, tonight you showed me another side to John Watson, and it was eye-opening."

"Oh, it's all in Doyle's brilliant story. Such a pity the playwright omitted Mary Morstan. My darling Watson has so few lines without her," said Brett.

At his recognition, I swelled.

"In the adventures, Watson has all the lines. He was created to tell the story! Why would that be left out? It is imbecilic! Surely, writers today can transpose descriptive monologue into dialogue."

He offered me a cigarette, which I declined.

Mr Brett lit another of his American cigarettes and savoured the smoke.

"John Watson is an everyman. He is the better character. It is a lot of fun to play Watson. He's a cheerful, kind, and loving individual who gets hurt and a little angry when his friend treats him or other people badly."

"You bring honour to the man. Through your portrayal, I can certainly believe in his boast of an experience of women which extends over many nations and three separate continents."

I nodded to the crowd of women waiting to enter.

"I see an amazing career ahead of you, Mr Brett."

Then finished my champagne, and we shook hands. I moved to go.

"But you have the advantage of me—" I heard Brett say as I stepped into the hallway and was lost in his lovely rose-bearing admirers.

My fourth time trip returned me to where it began. For my stability and the safety of Well's Time Machine, throughout my experiment, whenever I set foot in 1980 New York, I kept the same hotel suite and requested the same porter. Through the advantages time travel offers, my necessary accommodations were comfortably prearranged. The machine whizzing back and forth in time every day seemed not to distress it. On the contrary, it responded well to frequent use. Yet could not stay locked up as an attaché indefinitely. It was possible to rent a designated space in the hotel garage. I disguised the machine by having the outer shell of a Ford Club Wagon delivered to my rented parking spot. Much less expensive without the innards. Inside it, the Time Machine was securely locked away. And with access to electricity, I could come and go without being observed.

Mr. Smith was a tall, stately, African gentleman, originally from Zimbabwe, with impeccable manners and taste. We were eye to eye. He knew everything about New York and beat me unmercifully at cards. He well knew my stories and was witness to much of my rage at damnable Holmes.

The next morning, over our room service breakfast, he dealt out the cards.

"My son is a forensic scientist. You may want to talk with him about your Sherlock Holmes."

I surveyed the hand I was dealt.

"He is not my Sherlock Holmes!"

"Correct me if I'm wrong, Doctor Doyle, but I think the author who created him would be proud of what he has achieved in the world. That here in 1980, one hundred years from the time his characters met and moved into Baker Street, and 126 years from Holmes' birth, they would still be so celebrated. I imagine he would be even happier that they and their creator were immortal."

Mr. Smith turned up his cards.

I looked at him with a wary eye and threw down my hand.

"Smith, you are either a magician or a cheat!"

He laughed and pushed across a business card.

"My son's card, Doctor Doyle. NYU Medical is just across town. You might enjoy visiting one of the best forensic facilities in America. But anti-up before you go."

Surely serendipitous, their medical library could offer me research into the history of tuberculosis.

I called the number and explained to the young forensic gentleman what his father had shared with me. He invited me in immediately, and I cabbed to NYU Tisch Medical Center on First Avenue. It had an impressive research department, of which forensics was a part. I entered the lab to find my unreferenced quote etched into the glass entranceway:

"When you have eliminated the impossible, whatever remains, however improbable, must be the truth." [6]

He met me at the door.

"You're Doctor Doyle? Are you linked to Sir Arthur Conan Doyle?"

He indicated the quote.

"Put 'er there!"

I shook his hand.

"I am—his grandson. And you are Thomas."

"Call me Tom. My father's impressed with you, Doctor, and he isn't impressed easily."

He helped me into a lab coat, handed me gloves, and escorted me around forensic.

The laboratory was filled with tools, some of which I could hardly imagine their purpose. But the test tubes and pipettes Holmes was comfortable with were here. Damn, why is he still on my mind? Microscopes were larger and multi-lensed. Fingerprints were taken for granted, and it was much cleaner than Bart's. This was a great hive of gloved, white-coated, masked and goggled scientists, each hard at their tasks, many working as teams.

"Forgive me; I have never seen a lab like this."

"Any questions, just ask?"

I smiled as we walked to a table.

"Thank you. How do you test for blood?"

"Ha, ha, Doctor Doyle, is that a joke? The chemical formula for Sherlock Holmes's test for haemoglobin wasn't revealed in *A Study in Scarlet*. Do you know it?"

"Tom, I see you are an aficionado, like your father. He is a great man," I said. "Just do not play cards with him. I am grateful for his care of me while here. He has assiduously acclimated me to this new city."

"We leave traces of ourselves wherever we go, on whatever we touch," he said. "Our dean Lewis specialises in innovation." [7]

"But Dr. Doyle, my father says you've lost faith in Sherlock Holmes. How can that be? To you, he's family!"

"Lost faith is a nice way to say I detest him."

He sat me down at what he called a Binocular Polar Microscope and tutored me in its use.

"We use chemistry, serology, geology, botany, metallurgy, physics, photography, microscopy, trace evidence analysis, infrared examinations of documents, firearms, and tool mark detection. Other than infrared, Holmes used all of these, plus his knowledge of London and a century of crime. He was a one-man forensic lab. Doctor Doyle, don't you know we think of Sherlock Holmes as a mentor?"

He held up his index finger.

"The first, number one, to advance a science against crime. All those years ago, Holmes created crime scene investigation, and we still use his methods in modern-day forensics."

I took my eyes from the microscope and stood as he led me to a video spectral comparator.

"You do realise my grandfather created him, his method, and everything he ever said or did? It is to Arthur Conan Doyle that these accolades belong. And to the forensic scientist who inspired him, Doctor Joseph Bell. [5] Not to Sherlock Holmes."

"Everyone needs heroes, Doctor Doyle. Especially we who see the darkest aspects of life. He's one of the sharpest scientific minds of all time. The tools he used and how he used them made us want to become forensic scientists. Your grandfather gave us the coolest scientist of all time in Sherlock Holmes."

I could not believe what I was hearing! This was too much.

"How can you, with your scientific mind, not see you are talking about a character who lives only in the stories I wrote? He is a figment of my imagination and experience! This is outrageous!"

He looked at me as if I were a ghost or a madman.

"What did you say?"

Peeling off my gloves, I handed him the lab coat.

"Ah, um, forgive me. I write pastiche stories based on my grandfather's characters."

I grabbed his hand and shook it.

"You must have important business to attend to. Thank you for this tour. I am impressed with your laboratory, and Holmes would be, as well. But you would never be rid of him. After learning all this equipment, he would push your tools to their limits and beyond. Holmes would return whatever hour of the day he needed to use them and stay all night. Thank you for the kind gift of your time."

I left the lab and took the elevator down. Thinking, *This is something I cannot accept! Holmes does not deserve this praise. Doctor Bell and the true pioneers of forensic science, and I do!*

When the door swished open at the Medical Center Library, all such thoughts were forgotten. I stood agape in what could have been the Library of Alexandria! The knowledge contained here could make me the wealthiest doctor in 1894. Thankfully, I am an author, not a practising medical man, and no longer tempted by such things.

I quietly researched the history of tuberculosis and, in relief and recognition, broke out into laughter and apologised my way out the door. My next time trip would be to my alma mater, the University of Edinburgh.

Cabbing across town, I prepped the Time Machine and jumped to 1961. There I found myself in very familiar surroundings. Eighty years ago, I became a Doctor of Medicine at this respectable pile.

A meeting with Professor Crofton had been prearranged. He was testing a combination of Streptomycin, PAS, and Isoniazid as a way to cure tuberculosis. Throughout history, there have been many approaches to conquering this virulent disease, and this showed the best chance of success.

"Thank you for seeing me, Professor," I eagerly said as we shook hands.

"Anything for an alumnus, Doctor Doyle, with whom did you study? Edinburgh has had so many distinguished teachers. What I wouldn't give to have been tutored by the great Joseph Bell." He leaned back in his chair.

I thought, *Ah, how soothing is the Scots lilt to my ears, like coming home. Bell is still honoured, as he should be.*

"Professor Crofton, I hope you will forgive me. Time is of the essence. Recently, my blessed wife brought a new and valiant soul into the world and gave me a son. Eight months later, the woman who had been my most gentle and ardent supporter was diagnosed with incurable tuberculosis. I have devoted myself to finding a cure for this dreaded malady. I would like to learn more about your program and the medicine you have devised."

The Professor sat up, attentive to my description.

"Incurable! Such a pack of lies. Well, when this period of testing is completed, the world will know this scourge is now conquered."

I was sitting on the edge of my chair.

"Professor, how do I bring Mrs Doyle under your care?"

"Once the drugs are refined, they must be administered immediately. The sooner, the better. We use a unique combination therapy approach. If used from the outset, this completely cures TB."

"How long does it take?"

At his every answer, my spirits rose.

"She will have to be under this regimen for six months, as in a sanitorium."

"And would I, as a doctor, be entrusted with administering this therapy?"

"No one has ever asked me that before." He took a long look at me as if assessing my worth as a doctor and said, "As long as you work with us to study and learn our processes. I see no issue with that."

I shook his hand.

"Thank you, Professor, you have given me back my hope."

Now I knew my wife had a chance. These experimental journeys had at least accomplished her salvation. This diagnosis was the most crippling blow of our lives.

For a short time, I again became a student at Edinburgh. Most importantly, I learned that Professor Crofton's chemical combinations were available to me in 1894 Britain. I purchased the equipment required to make these compositions, as they were not available in my day, and packed them in the Time Machine.

Before another time trip, I toured the Hospital and found Joe Bell's portrait hanging in tribute to the great man. It had been difficult to work here without his presence. If I had named him Bell instead of Holmes, would he get the world recognition he deserved? Joe Bell would never allow it. I carried away memories of my dear friend into the Time Machine and vowed to write to him as soon as I returned.

On my sixth time trip, I travelled to Zurich, Switzerland, in the spring of 1948. Switzerland was one of my favourite places. The mountains and the crystalline snow had not changed since my time. But now, there were great ski resorts, which I believed my humble endeavours had a hand in encouraging into existence. It was tempting to don the new apparatus and throw myself down a mountain. But spring avalanches threatened, and my time was limited.

Doctor Carl Jung was an enlightened Swiss gentleman, a brilliant and creative thinker with piercing eyes that readily took you in and analysed you in a matter of seconds. *Like that cursed Holmes!* Only he didn't boast about it. He had surprisingly good sense for a man whose vocation was dreams and nightmares. As with Einstein, I did not hide from him. He was, of course, interested in Well's Time Machine, and I brought the splendid device to its full size for his study.

Afterwards, he sat me in a chair.

"Your Sherlock Holmes, by the way, I own every story you see there in my library. Why did you kill him and with such glee?"

He sat across from me.

"It is why I am here, Doctor Jung. To sort it out. My wife was diagnosed with incurable tuberculous in 1893. My time trips were to forestall the possibility of losing her to the disease. I was certain that in the future, a cure would be found. But hardly had I time to recover from this disaster in our lives when my father died.

"These two most horrible misfortunes, coming within sixty days of each other, each took out a knee as sure as a bullet. I had nothing to stand on. I had always solved whatever problem came before me. My strong shoulders and my keen mind could find the answer. But not here. I was a failure, more than that. I had no options, and I felt utterly lost."

Jung was looking directly into my eyes.

"Doctor Doyle, your father died of alcoholism in the Royal Edinburgh Asylum. Is this correct?"

"Yes. There was no other way. He was violent when in his cups."

"Of course, what other choice was there in the 1890s? In his cups? Was this a scientist's definition?"

"Just a colloquialism—oh."

"Doctor Doyle, you were propelled back into your childhood position of complete helplessness by these terrible events. It is normal for children who grow up this way to powerfully re-experience this helplessness when the alcoholic parent dies. But in Sherlock Holmes, you have accomplished what very few have. You created a new heroic archetype. And you can't kill off an archetype, as his fans prove," said Jung.

Now was the chance to tell my side of the story.

"I did what anyone would do on a sinking ship and threw out what was weighing me down. What I threatened to do for years suddenly became easy. It was all over in one brutal and murderous thrust over the Reichenbach Fall. As you said, I enjoyed this push immensely and put an end to my Sherlock Holmes stories. The last one, 'The Adventure of the Final Problem,' was published two months after my father's death. Free of Holmes's cursed effrontery, I could instead focus my time on writing literary, historical novels and, of course, my wife's healing."

"In your travels, have you reviewed your own future?" Doctor Jung said. "I shall not discuss your stories beyond 'The Adventure of the Final Problem.' Your ability to choose your own future must be preserved."

It was unnerving. The Doctor held his hands like Holmes. Was he doing it on purpose to watch my reaction? These psychologists were strange that way. Freud had me lie down on a divan with my back to him! I thought it insulting.

"Only in so far as to be astounded by the number of books I have yet to write and that my dream of immortality is a faite accompli," I said.

"Yes, achieved by Sherlock Holmes. Why did you want to entomb your gold mine when every story raises your level of living, keeps your family secure, builds your houses, and gives you the acclaim every writer craves?"

Spoken in calm, measured tones. Similar to how Holmes would speak to those of lesser intelligence.

"He is arrogant and keeps me from my important work," I said.

Doctor Jung leaned forward, raised his voice, and spoke with feeling.

"Arrogant? Do you expect me to believe you killed off your most famous and lucrative character for this, Doctor Doyle? Impossible!"

"Freud said something similar."

He smiled. "It is a story you tell yourself."

He reached out and patted my hand.

"I am aware our time is limited. This is a process that usually requires months or years to accomplish. My conclusions may seem incredible and upsetting to you at first. You are a highly intelligent man, and in time, I hope you will be able to process them in a way that results in your liberation. Now, will you share your dreams with me, Doctor?"

At last, this was why I was here. To learn from Carl Jung's advanced knowledge. What did I have to lose? I rattled off my nightmares. He read them like an open book. Nevertheless, it was unpleasant to be regarded like a spider pinned beneath his magnifying glass.

"Doctor Jung, are you saying that in killing off Holmes, I have become my own character?"

I thought, *This is preposterous fantasy!*

"You wrote it. Surely you know that death at the Reichenbach Fall is not the act of Sherlock Holmes. But the brainchild of Professor Moriarty," he said with Holmes's infuriating placid tone.

"I am Moriarty?"

"As a shadow in your dreams," he said with fingers steepled.

"And in my writing!"

"Yes, I have read, 'The Parasite.'"

He pointed to his library.

"Interesting the timing of this story, so soon after your 'Final Problem.'"

My voice rose. "Is it that obvious?" *My God, if my stories are so transparent, my career is finished!*

Doctor Jung reached towards me and lightly patted my arm, addressing the terror of my unspoken thought.

Calmly he said, "To me, yes. But, I have analysed your dreams, Doctor. You speak about Sherlock Holmes in Moriarty's voice: 'That cursed Holmes!' When in truth, Doctor Doyle, Sherlock is the embodiment of your valiant desires, your knight in gleaming armour created to protect you and all you love and has granted your greatest wish."

"No! He is a monster who devours my time and my writing. How can you help me if you choose him over me?"

I stood abruptly and paced his office.

Doctor Jung picked up a book, turned to a marked page and read:

"There is no lane so vile that the scream of a tortured child, or the thud of a drunkard's blow, does not beget sympathy and indignation." [8]

"The quote is from your story, 'The Adventure of the Copper Beeches, yes?' Have you ever received the gift of that blessed sympathy, Doctor Doyle?"

I angrily approached him.

"I am an author. This is the story of a father imprisoning his daughter to gain her inheritance. An ancient story. I am setting the scene and bringing in the horror. If you are going to hold me to every word I write, you might as well join the Sherlockians!"

"Doctor Doyle, why are you here?"

His conclusions unnerved me.

"You sound like Freud, again."

But there was nothing behind it and he knew it. I sat heavily in my chair.

"Doctor Doyle, where your fear is, there your task is. It is clear to me that killing Sherlock Holmes is the outward representation of your inner enraged child who at one time wanted to kill his violent alcoholic father. Perhaps during a beating? Or listening to the screams of a mother or brother?" He watched my face closely. "The man whose infirmity left

63

you, his wife, and his children to support themselves. You couldn't express it to your poor father, dying in an asylum."

He callipered my state as I absorbed every blow.

Jung continued, "Your rage at shouldering that responsibility you safely transferred to Mr Holmes. You made him an addict, like your father. Then you used your abundant talent to murder him spectacularly. You did so publicly before all his fans. As well as your shadow self, Moriarty. But they aren't dead, and Sherlock Holmes is not a monster, quite the opposite. Yet they can still torment you whenever your old childhood wounds are inflamed. This you must reconcile within yourself."

Simultaneously feeling confused and energised, I hoped in time the confusion would lift as I reviewed this day. I thanked Doctor Jung for his inestimable ministrations and fuelled the machine.

My seventh time jump flew me ahead with a new awareness, to say farewell to my friends in 1980 New York.

Doctor Jung reminded me I created Holmes and Watson to keep my coffers full, but they were also gallant knights fashioned to protect me. Possibly why, even with all his flaws, Holmes was so famous. I had created a believable modern-day knight. Without a doubt, my writing talent had everything to do with that!

Announcing my imminent return to England, I thanked and said farewell to my COA friends. My remaining funds were left to Smith, tucked into *The Complete Sherlock Holmes,* signed by the author.

"My dear Mr Smith,

Thank you, my friend. Your astute impersonation of Dr John H. Watson created a calm centre in my travels.

This should cover my losses."

Arcuan Doyle

The machine was prepared. My final time trip brought me in seconds to 1894. I was ready to fulfil my destiny.

The sight of Wells's patio and the brisk early morning air filled me with purpose. Fragrant spring blossom and birdsong greeted me. I firmly stepped down from the machine onto British soil and knew I was finally home. A home I now took with me wherever or whenever I went. I was not the same man who left here on that first time trip. My imagination and intuition, which I had in abundance, were tugging at my sleeve. I carefully cleaned Wells's miraculous machine. With his help, together we produced my wife's medicine from the future. Then I excitedly bicycled to my home in South Norwood to deliver the good news. For her, I had only been gone a few days. For me, it was an epoch.

H. G. Wells's friends gathered a fortnight later in his drawing-room, a psychologist, a young man, a physicist, the time traveller, and the bearded man. The author was missing. The fireplace was gently flashing, surrounded by the comfort of wood panelling and Persian rugs of the affluent Richmond, Surrey, English home. Dinner was long past, and the participants had moved on to brandy and conversation.

"Where is our author?" said the bearded man.

The young man said, "Yes, would we not love to know if he is writing another of his first-class Sherlock Holmes stories?"

Wells offered, "Doctor Doyle has urged me to convey his apologies. He locked himself away and is heartily writing a novel based on an old Dartmoor legend."

Doyle's words to me were, "I have a bookshop full of stories to pen!"

Sidney Paget The Reichenbach Fall.

In The Land Of The Living

"By the blessing of God I landed, torn and bleeding, upon the path. I took to my heels, did ten miles over the mountains in the darkness, and a week later I found myself in Florence, with the certainty that no one in the world knew what had become of me." The Adventure of the Empty House. [2]

Saturated with the sensation of blessed escape, I directed this energy to my quadriceps and sprinted higher into the protection of the Swiss Alps. My boots flew fuelled by the exquisite joy beneath the thought that it was over. Sherlock Holmes had conquered Professor Moriarty! It was the crowning moment of my singular career.

The cruel intrigue of his contemptible thrust-and-parry was done. What I had accomplished by uncovering the chinks in his armour, and the cursed exertions of exhuming one impenetrable lair after another. Again and again, I rushed after his guilty coat tails, only to uncover his underlings offered as sacrifice. On his false trails, the dead men's bones crunched beneath my feet. Yet, he knew exactly where I lived. Every light I shined into his malevolence went up in smoke, an illusion created by an expert. At last, I seized a single thread and followed it through a thousand cunning windings to him. Then I lured him here, offering myself as bait.

Face to face, it had been comparatively simple to rid the world of his evil. And it was concluded. In the thinning air of this steep climb, my sharp laughter rang through the surrounding forest. Done! Complete! Finished! Ha! Watson and I will keep them busy securing half of London's criminal force in the Yard's stockade.

Regrettably, I was stalled in this endeavour as Colonel Sebastian Moran followed close upon me, Moriarty's right hand and Britain's foremost hunter. I pushed my muscles to their limit, leapt Alpine stones and twisted tree roots, and ascended the formidable elevation through the densely knit trees. My route led from the Reichenbach Fall to the Grosse Scheidegg Mountain Pass through the high Alps that shall ensure my freedom. I reached the forest above the now darkening ridge and climbed further, knowing altitude was a weapon I could wield.

I extracted a map and compass from my pocket and confirmed my route. It showed a clear path due west from where I was standing, though I feared much of it was presently covered with snow. Before leaving Meiringen and the Englischer Hof, I had pocketed this map and my compass.

If you had eyes to see, my dear Watson, you could have added that knowledge to the trifles found at the fall and reached a somewhat different conclusion as to my whereabouts. Ah, Watson, fear not, this disappearance will be quick and Doctor and Mrs. Watson shall remain safe.

Mountaineers knew that what at first seemed enjoyable in sunlight became life-threatening at sunset. Even on the 4th of May, once the abundant brilliance from our glorious star sank below the high peaks.

My senses were acutely alert for that evildoer who could send boulders my way. I leapt up to a high pine bow. Swaying with the wind, I climbed higher as I surveyed both before and behind. From the latter direction, I could trace the movement of a group of travellers on the valley path, too far for me to discern if Moran was among them. Here there were many with his colouring. I picked out three men with rifles. He was hunting his prey, of that I was sure. My feet hit the path running. As the sun continued its descent, my anxiety increased. Each fleeing step led me away from a dangerous killer yet into the sudden death of cold exposure, altitude sickness, or the uncertainty of a plunge from unknown heights. There was no moon. Thankfully, an aurora borealis lit the sky that night. The green, gold and white auroras spread like fiery wings over the Mountains as eerie phosphorescent light illuminated the Grosse Scheidegg Pass.

I raced through the cold, deep night. Moran's valley path was more hospitable, with Swiss munificence all along the way. During the cold hours before daybreak, I stumbled half-frozen into the chalet of Tobias Branger, in the small mid-mountain town of Rosenlaui. Peter Steiler had recommended his guidance to Watson and myself, over our final breakfast at the Meiringen Englischer Hof. I acquired a sheep's wool coat, meals, and two nights' sleep, which greatly enabled my adjustment to mountaintop heights, a pipe and tobacco, and clear confirmation of my path through the towering mountains to Grindelwald.

My most significant purchase was a pair of skis and instructions. Travel by ski would swiftly conduct me above Moran. Carefully pocketing Madam Adler's sovereign and my watch, as recompense, I conferred my gold watch-chain. Branger was delighted with the trade and jabbered over lunch about the fortifications to his home that this would bring his family. When I fell sound asleep at the table, he showed me to a comfortable bed and I slept 'til daybreak's natural cacophony brought me 'round. After breakfast, we spent the day together on skis.

"Always wear your Gebirgsjäger goggles," Branger said. He was a good teacher, and I accomplished the basics, "On the flat, Holmes, you alternate your glide, like this. Up the hills, you jog. Slide down with feet together, and I will teach you to turn," He said. After my first plunge into the powder, he also taught me how to stop.

I slapped him on his broad back.

"Branger, you have said nothing about sailing down a snow-covered mountain."

"Yes." He laughed. "But you will soon discover it."

And we raced, jogging up to the next level of snow. Glancing into the valley, I noticed the sun flashing off what could be binoculars or a rifle aimed our way. I pointed this out to Branger and we moved out of range. "Keep sharpening your turns. By nightfall tomorrow, you will find a shepherd's hut near Schwarzwaldalp." He pointed west. "You may have to dig your way to the door, but there is always dry wood for the fire. Spend the night there." He said. We returned for another simple repast. I acclimated well to this high altitude, and with my new skill, I felt assured of my journey.

But upon our return, Branger's son, a fine lad of ten, with the same light colouring and kind-hearted smile as his father, recounted a story that froze the blood in my veins.

"Papa, when I was coming home from school, I met a tall man who slapped me hard."

"What did he look like?" I asked.

"He had a moustache and wore a wide-brimmed hat."

"Did he say anything to you before he hit you?"

"He asked me if I had seen a man like you, Mr Holmes. But I didn't answer him. That's when he slapped me."

"Did he say anything, then?"

"He demanded to know where I lived. I didn't tell him. He followed me for a way, but as I reached the heights, he turned back down to the valley."

I put my hand on his shoulder. "You are a brave lad. Branger, he should have a school holiday for the next few days. It is time for me to leave and I will draw the evil away with me. He is clearly following my progress from the lower pass, yet I am still far beyond his range."

At daybreak, Branger and I skied the westward trail. He was with me for a mile or more, then waved, performed a perfect kick turn and headed home to guard his family. The full sun on the bright snow was exceptionally radiant. I was grateful for my goggles. My mountain muscles rejoiced at this new venture. Once again I watched along the ridges, and skied ever higher, my attention drawn to signs of avalanche and my persistent stalker. As with Moriarty, I again played the decoy to a man with evil intent. Travelling the Kleine-Scheidegg, I skied the mountain tops through its highest pass.

In the certainty of my training, I let myself go. I was tearing down the pass in an exceedingly fortuitous way to navigate the mountains and, as long as the snow held, a surprisingly quick means of travel. I ascended and descended the edge of the slopes. Below me were the dark and forbidding black rock of snowless peaks.

At the mountain hut, I searched wide for signs of Moran, then checked my breathing and pulse, and found no sign of altitude sickness. As I dug my way in, the sun had set. I caught a glint of something, half a day behind and far below me, like a signal flash which disappeared with the setting sun.

Weapons at hand were my superior vision, my keen hearing, the quickness I was reacquiring as the mountains moulded my muscles, the agility on skis I had attained, a master's ability with fist, sword, stick, and baritsu. I practised using my poles and skis defensively. One would surely present a formidable cudgel in hand combat. It became an extension of my sword arm. Confident in my solutions, I enjoyed the dinner I had stored, packed my pipe for a smoke, stoked the fire, hung the teapot above it, and slept.

Sunrise, I travelled the verge of snow, my boots riding the mountain perimeter below my wooden skis. By 9 a.m., the clouds rose above the peaks. I had a clear view of the valley path and surveyed it with some care, yet found only my sure conviction that Moran was gaining on me. At 9000 feet above sea level, Mt. Faulhorn was my highest point. Reading the mountain and discerning my best route, I leapt off swiftly and soon was flying with the cold air burning my lungs. I pointed myself towards the civilised valley and its rail terminus below. My skis paralleled and rushing toward the pine-rimmed bowl created by these majestic giants and the man-made comforts of Grindelwald. Approximating to flight, I was free as a hawk.[1]

I stopped above Bussalp Mountain to survey my path and plan my final descent. Here the spring snow thinned, the black rock more prevalent. It was a steep mountainside with a dangerous cliff face. I leaned my poles against the rock and pulled my boots from the skis.

At the sun's zenith, there was a fall of stones behind me and I moved to confront. Moran had the advantage. The path was asperous and narrow. The villain leapt from above and knocked me over the precipice. I quickly caught his boot to stop my rolling down the treacherous incline. I noted he had no firearms; his sudden mountain climb and height were affecting his breathing. He had indeed stayed to the valley path as he was not acclimated to this altitude. I used him as a rappelling rope and he was kept busy, retaining his balance. As soon as I gained a secure foothold, I yanked him further, then leapt to my feet, reached and swung my ski, catching him squarely in the abdomen. He rushed at me like a wild animal, his chest heaving horribly as he tried to breathe in the oxygen-depleted air and smashed me up against the rock face. I recovered instantly and hit him with a solid left to the jaw and a powerful right-left combination to the diaphragm.

Airless and gasping, completely winded, he crumbled to his knees, and I secured him, wrists in front.

"I didn't expect to see you this far from London, Moran. What brings you here?"

Wheezing, "You. . . murdered. . . the professor!" His vicious eyes burned into me. "Your turn!"

"How so?"

He raised his head and gloated, "You. . . will be. . . hunted!"

I smiled, "A Swiss gaol is next for you, Moran. Extradition to London for a swift trial, and then you can join your beloved professor. But for now, a steep hike down the mountain."

He had nothing but a multi-plex knife, a night train ticket to Calais, and some bills. I admired his dogged determination to throw himself into the high Alps with such. We hiked down to the toboggan run for a less treacherous way into the valley.

In the guise of Sigerson, an explorer for the Norwegian Science Institute and speaking fluent German, I met with the Swiss Police at Grindelwald. Moran was locked in the gaol. The whole of the day was spent making my case clear against him and communicating with Mycroft via telegram. Once his uncharacteristically exuberant relief at my existence was past, he was supremely helpful. He prepared the Swiss authorities for the extradition of this wanted British criminal who had illegally concealed himself in their country for a dastardly purpose. I gained a new understanding of the extent of my brother's jurisdiction. At the foot of the Eiger, in the Hotel Gletschergarten, I dined and slumbered. Next morning, the Grindelwald Police insisted on escorting us to Bern. Moran, duly handcuffed and shackled, travelled with an officer of the law on either side of him, in our compartment on the Bernese Oberland Railway.

The Yard would only hear the ravings of a madman who had been exposed far too long to the elements. And since this undertaking would soon come to a close, it was of no concern. Moran cursed me as I left him in a Swiss gaol.

"You're a doomed man. Every one of my friends in every country, city, and town will lick their lips for a chance at Sherlock Holmes!"

"Ha! The same old song, so many have sung it."

I left the morose and scheming colonel behind. My day within the bureaucracy of Swiss justice was more wearing than all the mountains I had skied and again I was in awe of how well my brother cut through it. I put up for the night at Hotel Schweizerhof. The next day, I travelled by rail through the Southern Alps into Italy, and onward to Florence.

Mycroft had arranged for my abode at the St Regis, a bit more to his taste than mine, but his financial support was immediate and abundant. So my time in glorious Florence, when not catching up on sleep, was once again as comfortable as my rooms in Baker St. That was if everything in it was gilded! My first attention after arising from a glorious two-day slumber was to find a tailor. A most joyous pastime in Florence. I have never been so attired. I refurbished my watch-chain and Madam Adler's token was now adorned in Florentine fashion.

For a day, I indulged in recuperation in one of the world's most beautiful cities. If art was balm to the soul, mine had found its way to the supreme oasis. I know marble is metamorphosed and recrystallized in large veins in the ground. Nevertheless, Michelangelo's superb alchemy confused the senses into expecting his marble creations to be warm and pliable like the human skin and muscle they so perfectly impersonated.

Watson, I am keeping an occasional journal, so you might forgive this brief exodus.

Brother Mycroft sent tickets to my hotel for a performance of Verdi's Opera, La Traviata at La Pergola's Sala Grande. Handwritten on the back was one word: "Fermani." A dapper, young, and genial Italian gentleman entered the opera box and seated next to me.

"Mr. Holmes, I am Enrico Fermani, an emissary of your brother Mycroft, and molto felice to meet you." He kissed both my cheeks.

The instant he entered, I observed he had a revolver in his pocket, was a well-educated, and rather excited, local gentleman. I returned his greeting and discerned he also speaks truthfully.

"Mr Fermani, what do you have for me?"

"Mr Holmes, I have much to share and would ask you to visit me at my home, where we won't be overheard." He offered his card. "Mycroft was happy to hear from you, as was

I to find out you were still with us. If there is anything you require, I can obtain it for you," he said.

"Shhh. . . Fermani!" I held up my hand to halt conversation during the orchestra's overture and Luisa Tetrazzini's superb performance as "Violetta." I closed my eyes and connected with Verdi's mind. Fermani cried his way through it.

At intermission, he made use of his handkerchief. "I knew you had the heart of a musician, Mr Holmes."

"Unfortunately, my violin is in London."

"That can be arranged."

"When do we meet?"

"With your approval, immediately following the opera, I will guide you there. My home is in the hills, beautiful to see the sunset over the Arno from my home. The magic of Florence lives there."

He drove me to where the homes were clinging to the hillsides like the sheets of rock-roses adorning their walls. We climbed up to a large terrace. There we enjoyed a supper more exceptional than Marcini's can prepare and an admirable vintage.

"You have a fine home, Fermani," I said through my cigar smoke.

"Mr Holmes, your brother has given me a fine life. This work he asks you to do will not be easy. You will travel to places no Englishman can. And if discovered, your life or your freedom will be in jeopardy."

"Facts, Fermani! Where and why?"

"To Lhasa, Tibet, the Dalai Lama has been kidnapped. Mycroft wants you to find him, and by so doing, to establish a more positive relationship between Britain and Tibet. You must assess Tibet's true relationship with Russia. He is having some difficulty with the British Army and he wants to dissuade them from taking military action in that country."

"Isn't he a child?"

"The Dalai Lama is thirteen, an adult by some standards. Once you get into Lhasa, the rest will become clear."

"Do I consociate with the Russians, the Chinese?"

"There is a Russian Monk in Lhasa. A familiar of the Dalai Lama, defining this relationship is also your goal."

"I will find the boy. When did this happen? The ransom demands?"

"He was taken last night. No ransom note. How is this possible with hundreds of warrior monks around him?"

I waved his question away. "Most likely, his traces will disappear by the time I arrive. Nonetheless, the solution of a puzzle like this has many similar steps."

"You will be well provided for, but once inside Tibet, all safety will be gone."

"Surely they have telegraph?"

He shrugged. "Mr Holmes, I have made arrangements for you in India, where you will travel to Tibet with a knowledgeable guide for the strategic climb up the Nathu La Pass. I have a replacement for your lost gun." He handed me a box and boxes of ammunition.

"Ah, Webley Mark III .38. Thank you." I hefted, loaded, aimed and fired off a few shots, and pocketed it.

"It's no matter, Mr. Holmes. A lemon tree can be replaced. And I will help you find what you need for this perilous journey."

"Fermani, I am grateful for your assistance." I stood, and he hugged me like a brother. I stepped out of it and shook his hand. "Tomorrow morning, I will research my trip at the Institute of the History of Science library."

"Mr Holmes, I might recommend to you also, the National Central Library, on the Piazza dei Cavalleggeri."

"We shall meet there at noon."

I awoke to the newspaper story of Moran's foray into the channel as his ship left the French coast. Even in Italian, it was clear he had escaped. Met by a small fast boat that disappeared into the fog. Following my research, I checked out and travelled eastward.

On an island in the lake region, a man confronted me with a gun. I kicked it from his hand and demanded who sent him. He spat and leapt at me. I flipped and pinned him against the ground, his arms underneath, and my arm pressing on his throat.

He coughed out, "Holmes, you're a dead man, we will not stop, there are many more of us!"

I pressed harder, and he lost consciousness. I tied his hands and delivered him by boat to the Polizia di Stato. That night, I realised Moran's hand in this as another thug ambushed me on the beach in Bari. This time, my attacker did not yield and fired at me. I threw myself in the sand, rolled and shot him from a soldier's position. My search found only British cigarettes and bullets for his Enfield .47 pistol. Mycroft's plan looked to be my best. I would disappear to the one place in the world where none of Moran's assassins could find me.

I reached the HMS Turkey moored in the Mediterranean and boarded her, a mercantile shipper on an opium run. Our fast P&O vessel steamed across the top of the African Continent and through the Suez. The night was overcast and starless. A man rushed at me to sweep me overboard and I pulled my gun. He went for it and in the scuffle, the hair-trigger fired. He was pronounced dead by the ship's surgeon and I was locked in the brig. Once the ship left the Canal, my Arabian Sea voyage, locked in the bilge hold during turbulent seas, was not restful. Freed from the brig by Mycroft's cable, I then tanned my skin on deck. My natural colouring required no change.

No matter how difficult were the circumstances, my brother's support was readily available. I had hurled myself into the void. Traversed areas I'd only imagined half a world away. Vaulted off the comfortable edge of my London life and nowhere did I feel adrift, for the extent of Mycroft's reach was astounding yet, as his brother, rather comforting.

I disembarked in India at Kolkata and trained northward to Sikkim until I stood in complete awe at the foot of the Himalayas. Tibet sat upon a high plateau on the other side of the Nathu La Pass. I had underestimated Moran and killed two of his men to get there. I slept through my journey halfway across India dressed like a local. While curled up asleep, my height was not a problem.

For an Englishman, Tibet situated at the top of the world was impossible to obtain. We were forbidden to enter Lhasa. Yet the Russian monk was trusted. I grew a beard and spent my time climbing the Pass by learning to speak Russian and Tibetan. The muscles I had built in the Alps lamented over the long sea voyage and lounging in Indian trains. Primed for a challenge, I accompanied a caravan through the ancient Silk Road Pass. A party of Tibetans with sturdy mountain ponies packed our camp outfit. 14,140 feet above sea level, the road led through a dense pine forest which covered the Nathu La

Pass to its summit. Our guide was a Panaka Tibetan, clean-shaven with a quick mind and a well-muscled body. He carried a forty-four calibre Winchester carbine and vaulted onto his horse like an American Cowboy. I recognised Mycroft's sense of humour in this. We ascended the narrow trail, wound among the trees, and crossed the blue Tsomgo Lake. We slowly moved up the steep pass, given time to adjust to the altitude. At the apex, we reached the Chumbi Valley of Tibet and here parted ways. Mine led inexorably to Lhasa.

The beauty of the Alps united much of Europe, but the Himalayas were where God walked. Buddhist shrines greeted one all along the pass. Prayer flags multi-coloured, crisscrossed, and braided flew against the clear, knife-edged blue sky. My guide informed me that Tibetans tied flags and asked the mountain for, "One hundred years of life!" Fluttering in the sun, they led the way ever onward and upward. Here Mycroft had no help for me, a rupture in his world-sized net, and we were incommunicado. Yet there was no need, for I had entered Shangri-La.

At thirteen, Thubten Gyatso, the Dalai Lama, was a shrewd and intelligent young man. My research showed he was interested in political manipulation, peace, and power, and was a strong advocate for Tibetan independence. Yet was just as interested in world politics and what his part in it might be. He was a remarkable young man with a strong future in this pivotal region. I understood Mycroft's interest. The boy must be found. [2]

At the border, I was waylaid. My goods and pony were confiscated. I entered Lhasa not exactly as I had envisioned, but dragged in by the local authorities, speaking Chinese. It accomplished its purpose just the same. I was thrown at the feet of someone who had taken the place of the Dalai Lama, held at the end of many rather sharp sword points. A tall Russian monk recognised my English name and dismissed the guards. In Chinese, he addressed the figure on the throne.

"I'll take care of this aberration." He ordered me to rise and roughly brought me into a private room in the palace.

In Russian, I said, "Thank you, but you have the advantage of me." I put out my hand. He shook it.

"I am Agvan Dorzhiev, friend to the Dalai Lama. How may I help you, Mr Holmes?"

"You know of his disappearance?"

"It takes no great study to see that the boy on His Holiness's throne is Chinese."

"Would I be allowed to see his bedroom?"

"It is free." Then he spat on the floor, "The Qing imposter sleeps elsewhere."

"Now, sir!"

We walked to a high-ceilinged room filled with silk and brocaded wall hangings, in bright colours and intricate patterns. The accumulated scent of sandalwood incense was in the air and still in the boy's bed. The bed clothes and some of the hangings had been thrown and torn down as in a struggle. The windows had been opened and a few strands of straight black hair were stuck to the sill. Someone climbed up to this level and possibly exited with the Dalai Lama through this window. We went out and traced one set of footprints approaching the palace. He did not leave this way.

"Did you search the palace?"

"Yes. But the Potala Palace contains over 1,000 rooms. The Qing Chinese brought in their military who bared many of the doors."

"Can you make me a map of what was and was not searched in the palace? Immediately!"

We went to a small sparsely furnished room, his bedroom. He sat at his desk and created the map for me. I studied it.

"Do you have robes I might borrow? I will pose as a Russian friend and monk whom you are giving a tour of the palace."

He gave me an identical robe and as I dressed he said, "You don't know these guards, they—"

In Russian I said, "Time is of the essence, Dorzhiev. Follow me!"

We moved swiftly to the top floors of the Palace. There were no sentinels here. We searched every inch, and we descended in this way until a guard confronted us on the ground floor. Alcohol being a language spoken everywhere, I simulated a drunken state and offered him my bottle, encouraging him to drink his fill. Mixed with Watson's sleeping potion, we left him snoring at his post. We hunted through every room.

In this way, we descended to the lower floors and late into the night we finally happened upon a tunnel which led into hidden caverns carved out of the rock deep beneath the Palace. I quickly studied the marks left in the dust and discerned a struggle had taken place here. Then, guided by a faint scent of sandalwood, I found the locked door where we put two more guards to sleep. With a jemmy, Dorzhiev and I opened the stone door. Two jailers awaited us on the other side. I faced one, and the other faced Dorzhiev. It was a simple matter. We spoke the same martial language. Dorzhiev bowed to me and ran to the Dalai Lama, who was tied and bound in a chair, yet watched like a wide-eyed child.

Dorzhiev deftly untied him. I bowed, took out my knife, and cut through his bindings.

"Your Holiness, I am Sherlock Holmes, at your service."

"Mr Sherlock Holmes! You rescued me! And you, Dorzhiev, thank you."

"Your Holiness, there is more to accomplish."

I informed him of my simple plan. We three ascended past the sleeping guards to the Dojo and he rang the bell, calling all to meditation. The large hall filled with warriors, all of whom were ecstatic at the sight of the Dalai Lama. I explained my plan in Tibetan. In force, the Dalai Lama in the lead, with Dorzhiev on one side and myself on the other, surrounded by a hundred warrior monks, all of us sword in hand. We entered the palace throne room, with another fifty warriors at the doors.

Gyatso thundered, "Get off my throne you imposter! If you run fast enough, maybe my warriors will let you go!"

He ran out and was captured with all the Qing Chinese soldiers in the palace. Tibetan monks laughed them out the doors. The Chinese invaders were sent home with a message to not be so foolish again.

"His Holiness, 13th Dalai Lama has powerful friends and Independent Tibet is strong in his hands. We send your fools back to you in good faith, as Tibetans are a peaceful people!"

Following the monk's celebration and the sleep required to survive it. The young Dalai Lama and I argued the finer points of justice. He desired to prove to me the difference between Tibetan and English justice. But my view was a wider one and his awakening came when he realised that justice was a universal concept and right of all people.

Through the months I lived in the Potala Palace, I also taught him to play football. If the monks played in their dojo clothing, their robes were no hindrance. Three of the monks had come to Lhasa as young men in their twenties, so knew the game, and these became my Team Captains. Once we got the rules worked out, the Potala Palace monks enthusiastically took to the game. His Holiness used it to introduce the concept of democracy, as he shed his sacred accoutrements before every game.

"I like football, Mr. Holmes, but why did you teach it to us?"

"Because Gyatso, you are a man who is still a boy."

"Not to spread British values of democracy?"

"It seems to be effective."

"It is a different strategy from chess, but I think it also teaches battle skills."

"And teamwork."

"Yes, I do enjoy being able to depend on my teammate's abilities to win a goal." He stood straighter and raised his head haughtily. "In real life that doesn't exist, I make my decisions alone and my people accept them because the Dalai Lama makes them."

"You can also build a team to support you, Gyatso. That way, the growth of Tibet is shared."

"Like England. But won't my people forget me? Forget who I am?"

I smiled at his earnestness. "No one could forget you, Gyatso! Nor would they want to. You are an intelligent and insightful young man and will grow to be a wise leader. Your training in logic surely will show you that Tibet will still seek your judgment."

We walked from the White Palace to the Dojo.

"We British view the Queen as our supreme ruler, yet we also have a Prime Minister and an exceedingly active parliament."

"How long does all this take?" he said impatiently.

"That's where the teamwork comes in. The American Colonies accomplished it in seven years without the telegraph. Tibet can expeditiously achieve this goal. I have no doubt your leadership will carry the ball."

We entered the Dojo. I bowed to him, like a proper Englishman. The monks laughed heartily at this.

"They will teach you how to bow like a Tibetan." He laughed.

With a scientist's interest, I lived among them and was taught meditation by the Lhasa monks. There had been claims made by fakirs and priests as to feats of strength and pain carried out under meditation. Most of these claims fell apart once the light of science shined upon them. And yet, I became my own experimental subject. Imagine a weapon in my arsenal that disregarded pain. We spent full days chanting and meditating from morning to night. At first, my height was an obstacle to temple life during their extremely active prayer. But never in martial arts training, the smallest among them would undo me every time and laugh while doing so! They were lethal, yet enjoyed their lives to the fullest. The Monks drank me under the table, put me to bed and did it again the next night. You would fit right in, Watson.

While I was attempting to fuel my arsenal, I did not learn how to ignore pain. Yet my senses became stronger, my stance surer, and my fine hearing so attuned that even the monks could no longer surprise me. And I did acquire the incomparable gift of meditation.

Meditation and Martial Arts slowed the world down, almost like stopping time, and sped up one's reflexes. Until one became weightless, empty, and free. I had never been so awake!

Forgive me, ole boy. Though I believe this unfocused focus could be scientifically taught, this was something science could not give me.

The next day after our football game, Gyatso and I walked into the palace garden. In the centre a pool filled with blooming lotus.

He said, "From darkness and mud, perfection emerges.'3 That is Buddhism in six words. Mr. Holmes, it is my sincerest wish to lead Tibet in peaceful times, but my dreams are not peaceful."

It was time for me to address Mycroft's concerns.

"Gyatso, would I be permitted to speak again with your Russian friend, Dorzhiev?"

"He is a scholar and an earnest Buddhist monk who has great devotion to me, like you, Mr. Holmes." [3]

I lit my pipe.

Through the smoke, I said, "And Russian!"

"If by that you mean Russia influences me, you are wrong. I am interested in a good relationship with Russia, as I am with China, India, and Great Britain. These are my neighbours." He stopped and turned to me. "You know me well. Why do you question me?"

"It is my business. Thank you, Gyatso. But is Dorzhiev as sincere?"

"Dorzhiev is easy. Tomorrow he visits from Drepung Monastery. He will address your concerns as I have. Tibet wants to be an independent country, and it is my wish to fulfil that desire, but her relationship with her powerful neighbours is always uncertain. You have seen first-hand an attempt at invasion. And I thank you again for your intercession on my behalf. Mr. Holmes, how is it an Englishman without political aspirations is now involved in politics half a world away?"

I laughed. "Most British gentlemen have no such aspirations, Gyatso, only to rule benevolently within their private lives. I am my own man and other than my brother and my good friend Watson, have no affiliations. I am free to choose my work, my clients, my travel, and my friends."

"You are also my friend."

"And a most grateful one, Gyatso."

We sat cross-legged on fragrant, light wooden benches in the shade.

"When you ascend to the throne of Tibet, and if you create a similar form of democracy, you will make this possible for your people. And they will each define freedom." I said.

"But you pay taxes, bow to the Queen?"

"I give all gladly for the overriding protection and growth of my country. I see London as my small jurisdiction. Occasionally, other European cities or their Royals reach out for my help, publicly or in secret, as you are casually doing. In addition, the Queen is a very exceptional lady, and I bow based on how well she leads her empire." He looked at me questioningly, his young, intelligent face clouded with misunderstanding.

"I bow to England, not Victoria. That may be one of the ways Tibet differs from England. Gyatso, lead your subjects well, with intelligence, justice, and love, and they will always be ready to defend you and Tibet."

"I hope you are right, Mr Holmes. I am not sure if English democracy is as easily translated into Tibetan culture as football."

"My boy, I don't envy your future. Your choices are hard ones, but the world will know who you are, as will your people. And by your hand, they will be freed."

"You sound so sure."

"I see a solidly qualified leader maturing before me, a young man of supreme intelligence who will face his opportunities as a warrior of peace."

In his formal hall, we ate dinner with our football teammates, the conquering heroes. Dorzhiev explained their style of toasting, "Here wine is tasteless without song. You drink mellow Qingke while we, your hosts, sing toast songs to you." His Holiness and I drank and our team sang our praises. My blushes dear Watson.

The next morning, Dorzhiev and I met again. He brought me a lotus flower and bowed. I shook his hand and spoke to him in Russian.

"Mr Dorzhiev, I am grateful for your inestimable service in solving His Holiness's mystery. But there is more I desire to know. What is your exact relationship with Gyatso?"

Without affectation, he stated as fact, "He is my spiritual master, the Dalai Lama."

"Do you represent Russia in Tibet?" I said.

"Do you, Mr. Holmes, represent Britain in Tibet?"

"I do always, wherever I am," I said.

"So you are here as a spy or to influence His Holiness?"

"Neither! I came here to locate and liberate Gyatso, as I have done. Yet to alleviate the tension that exists between our two countries, I would also bring back to England Tibet's political reality. Can you help me to do so?"

"Mr Holmes, I know you are a gentleman of honour and your handling of His Holiness' horrible imprisonment was miraculous. I will help you in any way I can."

He declined the cigarette I offered, and I lit one myself. He concurred with the Dalai Lama's concern over Tibet's geographically imposed peril. I was convinced by his earnestness and lack of guile.

"I am afraid Gyatso may need your protection, and I ask you to remain close to him. He knows how to reach me in troubled times, yet my aid cannot be as expeditious as yours. His monks also protect him, but one man may sometimes do what an army cannot."

"In this, we think along similar lines, Mr Holmes. I am capable of what you ask."

"Do you see a Russian political or military influence in Tibet?"

"You are persistent on that subject, but it is merely a fantasy in the minds of Britain. No, I see the Dalai Lama and the Potala Palace and a peaceful, independent Tibet. As this is Gyatso's wish, I work to fulfil it. Today he wants to study Buddhism and leave leadership for his future self. As we believe:

"Men who have not gained spiritual treasures in their youth perish like old herons in a lake without fish." [4]

Dorzhiev continued, "But as you experienced first-hand, Qing China is like the hungry tiger that constantly tests our boundaries."

"Who is leading Tibet?"

"As usual, the monasteries wield great influence through the Regent," he said. "His Holiness wants to temper that, too. They serve Tibet and only Tibet. They are ignorant of the world and believe in myths, a dangerous view in these times."

'The world is on fire and every solution short of nirvana is like trying to whitewash a burning house.' Lord Buddha said.'" [5]

"Forgive my impertinence, Your Holiness, but whitewash is mostly water and holds within it the possibility of saving that burning house. The 13th Dalai Lama has appeared at the right time. He is a wise and courageous young man. I look forward to his leadership in the world," I said. "Do you foresee any dilemmas for Gyatso, besides his monstrous dreams becoming reality?"

"The major struggle for monks, especially when we are young, is to avoid four things: desire, greed, pride, and attachment. Of course, no human being can do this completely. Gyatso at thirteen has been practising meditation for seven years and as he grows to adulthood will conquer them." [6]

I acknowledged the similarity to my preferred style of living and asked about the means they used to rid themselves of such desire and attachment.

"We are taught to stare at a statue of the Lord Buddha and absorb the details of the object, the colour, the posture, the gentle face, and so on, reflecting on all we know of his teachings. Slowly, we go deeper; we visualise the hand, the ear, and other details, closing our eyes and trying to travel inward. The more we concentrate on a deity, the more we are diverted from worldly thoughts." [7]

"Ha!" I laughed as I recognised it. "Please forgive me, but you have just described my scientific method as a spiritual practice. Thank you, Dorzhiev."

I shook his hand, and we went laughed into dinner together. He sat on one side of Gyatso with me on the other.

The next day, I packed to leave. His Holiness and I spent a few last moments together.

"Gyatso, you have knowledge and desire for true justice for Tibet. Now you stand on the threshold of acquiring the experience that will bring you a man's wisdom."

He said, "Mr Holmes, your gifts of how a gentleman thinks, our talks, and even football. I feel will serve Tibet well in the coming years. You are a great friend to me and my people."

"Keep your martial arts senses keen and your sword arm awake, Your Holiness. I am always at your disposal by letter or wire to my brother Mycroft." I looked him eye to eye. "Stay close to Dorzhiev, especially in times of trouble. I thank you for your hospitality and the amaranthine gift of meditation. It has increased my ability to keep my mind open, objective, and of better use to me."

I bowed as one does in the East, forehead to the floor to the Dalai Lama. He immediately raised me, then shook my hand as an equal, wrapped a white silk scarf around my shoulders, and I left. I admit, much touched by his expressions of friendship and love.

Thubten Gyatso was positioning for political ascension. For good or ill, I had done much to dispel his distrust of the British. I cabled to Mycroft information which I hoped would put an end to our military's aims in this country. The Dalai Lama knew he could rely upon the Holmes brothers for personal intercession. It was time for me to leave. My enlightening idyll was over. In a few years, he would gracefully take the reins of his beloved Tibet in the midst of brutal and trying times. [8]

To facilitate my brother Mycroft's peaceful aims, I adopted the pseudonym Sigerson, an explorer with aspirations. To solidify my alias, I engaged the media with my tales of Shangri-La. *Surely, Watson, you could read between the lines.*

Sigerson shot off an article to a most valuable institution, the International Geographic Society's Journal. Until it was prudent for Sherlock Holmes to return to London, Sigerson's explorations would embellish his legend as he travelled into strange and mysterious lands where no Englishman could go.

Holmes and Watson by Frederic Dorr Steele

A Watsonian Conundrum

Holmes & Watson on Censorship ala "The Field Bazaar"

Sherlock Holmes and Doctor Watson were at the fire, smoking their post-dinner pipes. Holmes opened a thin green-backed journal and quickly read through it, lit his pipe, and then addressed Watson.

"My dear fellow, it says here, I am not allowed to talk with historical figures, nor consort with women, or dance, nor play any of the music of the twentieth century! I do so love Gershwin and Ives. You know, for introspection, the Americans have topped the Germans. Watson, this is appalling! Could these people actually have the ability to curtail my life this way?"

"Holmes, let me see that. It's *The Watsonian* journal. What's this, a journal in my name? If it wasn't so funny, I'd cry. Maybe I should sue?"

"Watson, it says I deviate from canonical convention if I don't follow these rules. The author quantifies how many times I took tobacco from my Persian slipper, that I laughed most in 1887, how many times I wore my dressing gown and which colour, even where your war wounds are! This is a serious idée fixe. Might even be mono mania. What do you say, Doctor?" He looked around. "Watson?"

Watson ran up the seventeen steps to the sitting-room, returning from a phone call.

"Holmes, I'm all set. I've engaged my solicitor, Clarence Darrow. He thinks it's a joke, but might be worthy of a suit."

"A man after my own heart."

"Holmes, you have railed against Scotland Yarders who have no faculty of imagination and shared with me that in your estimation it is one of the principal ingredients for a successful detective. I find it is also necessary for a successful author."

"Your success as an author is not in doubt, Watson. You do have some facility for imagination on the page, my friend."

"It is one of the greatest accomplishments of an author to inspire his reader's imagination. We can read the same story and because of the miracle of our uniqueness, it lights up our imaginations differently. But you mentioned famous historical characters, Holmes?"

"Yes, this composition asserts that under no circumstances have you used them in your chronicles, but my memory serves up something else."

"Holmes, are you sure this is about my stories? Right from the start, *A Study in Scarlet*, I brought famous, historical characters into it: Joseph Smith and Brigham Young. These men are considered religious prophets: you can't get more famous than that! My stories are Non-Fiction, accurate chronicles of your cases. Not some imaginative fancy. Their association with the Mormons endangered and compromised my characters' lives."

"I don't think I've told you how proud I was of that one. Your first and one of your best."

"Thank you, Holmes. In the 'Five Orange Pips,' I cast a historical and very real organisation, the Ku Klux Klan, as the villain. I even described how their name came about."

"I think we can agree, Watson, that you are a courageous gentleman who rarely steps away from a good fight."

"The story of the scourers of Vermissa Valley, Pennsylvania, is about a real place, a real-time, and a real people. The Pinkerton National Detective Agency is featured in two of my stories. It was established in the United States by Scotsman Allan Pinkerton in 1850, around the assassination of President Lincoln. It employed women and Africans from its founding and became the largest private law enforcement organisation in the world."

"I have a high regard for the Pinkertons."

"In 'The Adventure of the Second Stain,' I placed a notable person in the centre of the story. A main character and referred to as Prime Minister throughout. Everyone knows William Ewart Gladstone is the PM. It's his 4th term! I didn't think it was necessary to spell it out. Yet, I will admit that in my usual way of preventing a libel suit, I camouflaged him slightly by labelling one of the most liberal PMs in British History, a conservative."

Holmes in his bedroom was exchanging his mouse grey dressing gown for white tie.

"I think you have thoroughly made your case, Doctor. So, shall we go dancing? There's a Cinderella Ball at the Langham Hotel tonight, and a bevy of American beauties has recently disembarked at Southampton. Watson, get dressed!"

Crown Rose, British Library Archives.

Miss Annie Harrison's Rose Soliloquy

21 February 1894,

Dear Doctor Watson,

I write this to express my sympathies for the inconsolable loss of Mr Sherlock Holmes. The innocent people of Britain have lost their great protector.

As Mr Holmes's biographer, please contact me about any changes you deem necessary in the enclosed manuscript. It is to be published in *The Serpentine Muse* as it touches upon issues of interest to women.

It is my hope these thoughts will bring back happy memories for you.

What a lovely thing a rose is.
There is nothing in which deduction is so necessary
As in religion.
It can be built up as an exact science by the reasoner.
Our highest assurance of the goodness of Providence
Seems to me to rest in the flowers.
All other things,
Our powers, our desires, our food,
Are really necessary for our existence in the first instance.
But this rose is an extra.
Its smell and its colour are an embellishment of life,
Not a condition of it.
It is only goodness which gives extras,
And so I say again,
That we have much to hope from the flowers.

As fiancé, now wife, to one of Mr Sherlock Holmes's illustrious clients, my relation to the great detective is a unique one. It is now two years, and along with all of Britain, I continue to mourn the loss of Mr Holmes.

The ideas in this letter are offered as an addendum to your *Strand Magazine* chronicling of Mr Holmes's successful case entitled, "The Adventure of the Naval Treaty."

Readers of your stories know that Mr Sherlock Holmes recited the above poem following my husband, Percy Phelps's, recounting of the disastrous events which lead to his long illness. I was present at the recitation of this verse. It impressed me, as the detective clearly improvised it on the spot.

Doctor Watson, you have stated elsewhere that Mr Holmes was a gentleman who believed:

> "The motives of women are so inscrutable. How can you build on such a quicksand? Their most trivial action may mean volumes, or their most extraordinary conduct may depend upon a hair-pin or a curling-tongs." The Adventure of the Second Stain.

Of course, I could not agree with this sentiment. Dismissal of the whole of womankind like this was appalling. The accomplishments of Miss Nightingale alone surely disproved it. She has competently shown us how important was the nursing profession and I took such work very seriously.

To achieve his ends, it seemed there was nothing that Mr Sherlock Holmes could not do. Some have said his impromptu

Rose Soliloquy showed his inquisitive power as a deep thinker and lover of beauty. Others have waxed poetic over the passage, conferring upon him the roles of dreamer and philosopher.

From our association during the search for the Naval Treaty, I know that Mr Holmes might well encompass this and more. As he might say, genius was not limited by the commonplaces of existence. From your stories, Doctor Watson, I know Mr Holmes was a lover of musical beauty, precise language, and art. He appreciated the elemental beauty of the science of chemistry and his ability to work within this invisible-made-visible world. Occasionally he even admitted to an appreciation of gentlewomen:

> "She was a lovely woman, with a face that a man might die for." A Scandal in Bohemia.

> "You seem to me to have acted all through this matter like a brave and sensible girl, Miss Hunter. Do you think that you could perform one more feat? I should not ask it of you if I did not think you a quite exceptional woman." The Adventure of the Copper Beeches.

How would one explain such a seeming departure from the clarion logical mind of Mr Sherlock Holmes? We could compare the Rose Soliloquy with similar departures. Another of these also occurs in "The Adventure of the Naval Treaty."

> "Look at those big, isolated clumps of buildings rising up above the states, like brick islands in a lead-coloured

sea. . . Lighthouses, my boy! Beacons of the future! Capsules, with hundreds of bright little seeds in each, out of which will spring the wiser, better England of the future."

Then there is Mr Holmes's unique speech on the London docks in *The Sign of Four*.

"How sweet the morning air is! See how that one little cloud floats like a pink feather from some gigantic flamingo. Now the red rim of the sun pushes itself over the London cloud-bank. It shines on a good many folk, but on none, I dare bet, who are on a stranger errand than you and I."

Doctor, you have faithfully reported Mr Holmes's philosophy of life and shared this with us throughout your excellent biographical stories. Yet, it seemed to me that all but the Rose Soliloquy were instances spoken to you alone. Possibly because of my involvement, I believed the purpose of the Rose Soliloquy was different. It was recited to the three other inhabitants of the sick room, of which I was one.

In my extracurricular research on the subject, I found both inanity and scholarship. There was the suggestion that Mr Holmes might have been influenced by cocaine during this Soliloquy. As a nurse, I am pleased to affirm that Mr Holmes was completely free of chemical influence throughout the solving of our case. Doctor, you stated in 'The Adventure of the Yellow Face':

"He only turned to the drug as a protest against the monotony of existence when cases were scanty and the papers uninteresting."

A horrible practice! One would hope such an intelligent gentleman could find a better way through the monotonous periods of life. The joys of gardening, perhaps, or charity work?

My further research uncovered some rather unsettling statements claiming the Soliloquy proved Mr Sherlock Holmes's conversion to various religions. Mr Holmes, the man of science, has repeatedly overthrown such ridiculous sentiments himself.

"I see that you have quite gone over to the super-naturalists. But now, Dr Mortimer, tell me this. If you hold these views, why have you come to consult me at all?" *The Hound of the Baskervilles.*

Mr Holmes's view of his clients was especially appropriate here. Starting with *The Sign of Four*:

"It is of the first importance,' he said, 'not to allow your judgment to be biased by personal qualities. A client is to me a mere unit, a factor in a problem. The emotional qualities are antagonistic to clear reasoning. I assure you that the most winning woman I ever knew was hanged for poisoning three little children for their insurance-money, and the most repellent man of my acquaintance is a philanthropist who has spent nearly a quarter of a million upon the London poor."

To you and Mr Holmes, I was the only unknown in Percy's bedroom. Even though Percy was my only focus, Mr Holmes's departure from the events of that day was accomplished by one of the flowers I had used to create a cheery convalescent room. There was no doubt in my mind what he meant by picking that rose.

In his defence, during Mr Holmes's visit to Briar Brae, he had no chance to speak with me. He had interviewed my brother and now Percy, but had no chance to do so with me. I was completely devoted to Percy in my dual roles as nurse and fiancé.

Even after Mr Holmes had successfully ascertained my character to his satisfaction, he then had only one rushed moment available to involve me in his plan. For Percy's sake, I instantly complied. After all, as strange as Mr Holmes's methods seemed to us at the time, he was our only hope. I have since forgiven his unmanly silence as to my dangerous task. The poor man must have been beside himself to introduce the rose as a ruse.

Percy's sick room, as you painted it, Doctor Watson:

"With flowers arranged daintily in every nook and corner. The open window, through which came the rich scent of the garden and the balmy summer air."

I imagine that along with everyone else who could read in Great Britain, Mr Holmes had heard of the popular poem, "The Romance of the Rose." I certainly had. It professed courtly romantic love and equated women's 'charms' with the beauty of the flower. This old-fashioned view of women was written in medieval times. Here is a segment:

Who gave you, beautiful child,
This freshly blooming flower?
What a shine, what a sweet smell!
Among this radiant garden
That the Dawn blooms every day
On its green stem,
Still sparkles a tender tear,
And there, on its half-opened lip.
It is she who is so precious
And so worthy of being loved,
That she must Rose be named.

Whether Mr Holmes knew of this poem, his improvisation on the nature of women could have been inspired by similar references to the rose from the worlds of theatre, music, and religion. For example, Robert Burns' poem, or Tchaikovsky's waltzes. An ancient line from a poem by Haviz: "How did the rose ever open its heart and give to this world all its beauty?" These he most likely called to mind when creating his Rose Soliloquy.

When Mr Holmes walked into Percy's sick room that day, he must have observed how beautifully I redecorated it with blooming summer flowers and roses. As I was preoccupied with Percy's constant care, I hoped they were well placed to cheer him. Yet, I could not have realised how our relaxed relationship after ten weeks of nursing would seem to two London gentlemen. How our casual comfortability with each other might seem quite improper.

After all, we met in Percy's bedroom. I was sitting close to him, holding his hand, and even though I was his nurse, I was also his fiancé. I was much more familiar with my charge than say, the night nurse. In my worry as to how Percy would fare during this meeting, I was literally attached to him. As Percy's nurse, it would be improper and possibly unhealthy to wrest my attention away from him. Not that I would permit it!

Doctor, as you know, the rules governing the relations between single women and bachelors were strict moral codes. The two that applied here: A single woman never addressed an unknown gentleman. Nor could she converse with a gentleman without being formally introduced. There were many others, yet I am sure these sufficed to bring Mr Holmes to his poetic solution.

Therefore, the situation as he saw it would not allow Mr Holmes to interview me. He wanted answers: *Was she innocent of the crime? Where do her loyalties lie? Was she in on it? Was she the villain or the sister of the villain? Was she playing Percy, or was her devotion true?*

Neither Percy nor I knew Mr Holmes before that day. Of course, we knew of him and his abilities thanks to your stories, Doctor Watson. We hoped his involvement in our predicament would bring similar success. There was so much at stake. When he improvised the Rose Soliloquy as flypaper masked in profundity, we did not know what to think. He started with a radical equation combining science, nature, and religion as a sure way of gaining an intelligent woman's attention. He propounded his theory that flowers, especially roses, were extras and therefore proof of the generosity of Providence. Twice, stating that this offered hope to us all.

The scientist, Mr Holmes, probably knew of Hofmeister's 1851 proof of the sexual life of plants as their purpose in nature, but turned his poetic references in a different direction.

The suspending of your judgement was now requested and your forgiveness over my seeming egoism. I was sure the Soliloquy was not about a rose at all but was intended to capture the attention of the only woman in the room.

Mr Holmes's thinly disguised queries were cloaked in roses. He began by addressing me (the rose.) Then introduced himself (the reasoner.) He ended by emulating the poet of "The Romance of the Rose" in praising the flowers as if they were me.

> "But this rose is an extra, an embellishment of life. It is only goodness which gives extras. We have much to hope from the flowers."

What little he knew about me, he deduced from his glances around the room. A woman engaged to be married, with faith in the curative properties of flowers, plus my nursing gifts to Percy over these many weeks. The rules of etiquette for unmarried men and women were very clear. Mr Holmes could never address me directly unless I was properly introduced to him beforehand.

Percy's mentioning my name in passing, "If it had not been for Miss Harrison here and for the doctor's care, I should not be speaking to you now," is not a formal introduction.

As my remaining during Percy's meeting with Mr Holmes was a last-minute request of my fiancé, neither my brother nor Percy thought to do so. If they had introduced us, only then could Mr Holmes speak directly to me, and only if I permitted him. Because we met in Percy's bedroom, the carefree relationship between Percy and myself, and the propriety of formal rules stymied him.

Instead, Mr Holmes chose to elicit my compliance with poetry. Poetry is one of the few allowed reading materials for young ladies of my day. I understood his message immediately and brazenly confronted him in the role of Percy's nurse defending the sick room.

At the end of the Soliloquy, Mr Holmes seemed to be lost in thought. For me, it was endearing to witness the Great Detective at a loss, even for a few moments. It was this show of humanity, his devotion to solving Percy's mystery, and his acknowledgement of my intelligence, which resulted in gaining my compliance on his next visit.

Though Mr Holmes battled daily in the dark alleys of murderous crime, I realised he still saw beauty in the soul of man, and most of all, in his pursuit of true justice. This, I now knew, was the actual purpose behind his Soliloquy.

Without costume or anonymity, Mr Holmes used his acting skill and love of language to transform the empiricist into a romanticist. And as I was about to discover. It was Mr Holmes's way to draw out a client by nonchalantly turning his back on them.

Now we must return from our reverie and recall that above all, in "The Adventure of the Naval Treaty" Mr Sherlock Holmes was solving a puzzle with very serious consequences. The threat of war in Europe, let alone Percy's career. As always, Mr Holmes would do whatever he could to gather all the information he needed to arrive at the solution.

He would even appear the rose-besotted fool. Therefore, he used his considerable touch of the dramatic and his understanding of the symbology of the rose to separate the fiancé from the nurse and overcome my stalwart protection of Percy, if only for an instant.

It was an honour to observe Mr Holmes at his most daring, going into battle with a rose, his only shield. This time, he wasn't facing a godless murderer. He was encouraging a woman's wrath. Afterwards, Doctor, he revealed what he had learned from his gamble:

> "She is a good sort, or I am mistaken. She carried out every one of my injunctions to the letter, and certainly without her cooperation you would not have that paper in your coat pocket."

And true to form, in the next instance, Mr Holmes enlisted me in the springing of his trap. I was grateful to have helped him in restoring the honour of my family by foiling my wayward brother, and thereby bringing health and prosperity to Percy.

Thank you for your generous attention, Doctor. I thank providence every day that Percy had the courage to reach out to you and your associate for help. For where would we be without it?

Ever Sincerely,
Annie Phelps, née Harrison.

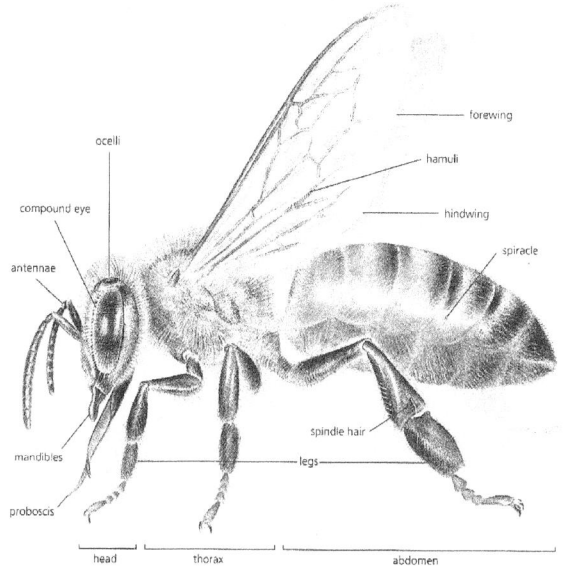

Anatomy of the Bee. [1]

Mrs Hudson's Garden

"How quiet and sweet and wholesome the garden looked in the moonlight." The Adventure of the Engineer's Thumb.

The twelve-page monograph presented here exhibits the wisdom and abundance of the timeless Welsh proverb, "A seed hidden in the heart of an apple is an orchard invisible."

Recommendations from the Arts and Crafts Gardeners will be our guide as to how to encourage that seed and many others to grow. My 60-foot square London cottage vegetable garden is an example of what good can come from applied knowledge and the joyous effort of friends working together towards such a satisfying goal. [2]

Some subscribe to the idea of the green-thumb, that they are lacking and unsuited to grow food. Pooh! Green-thumb or purple-thumb, I agreed with the poet, Thomas Moore, who said, "A piece of sky and a chunk of earth lie lodged in the heart of every human being." [3]

The Garden Wall

You may be pleased to note that some roses are, in fact, evergreens. In these Isles, we celebrate roses in profusion 'til December and beyond.

It is reasonable to dress our garden walls with whatever we decide will look the best. For me, hardy varieties work well. We have trained Piccadilly and November Roses to climb as high as is possible and added clematis for early contrast.

Plant November Roses at the wall. Train carefully. Bend only as each cane's direction permits and anchor them onto the wall. They will require pruning and redirecting. This process will take many seasons, yet its result is well worth the effort. Piccadilly and other varieties of climbing roses require less exertion, as it is in their nature.

Morning Glory and honeysuckle are other yet wilder choices. They will run up a wall of their own accord and will occur where they may. To be greeted by the brilliant, trumpeting Morning Glory is its own delight.

I wish I had been in a fly on the wall of that flower arranged sitting-room where Mr Holmes opined on the nature of roses, "This rose is an extra. Its smell and its colour are an embellishment of life, not a condition of it. It is only goodness which gives extras, and so I say again that we have much to hope from the flowers." [4]

It was a sunny and warm for winter day when Doctor Watson joined my gardening enterprise. He was clearly looking for something to do as Mr Holmes had been entertaining clients in their sitting-room all morning. The good doctor passed through my kitchen and opened the garden door.

"Good morning, Mrs. Hudson, beautiful day," he said.

"Oh yes, it is, Doctor. I hope you like your new accommodations. Those stairs do not vex your injuries?"

"Thank you, no, Mrs. Hudson. They are therapeutic."

I looked up at him. "What do you think of my little garden?"

"It seems well-organized for January."

Chuckling, I said, "It is that. In a month or two, you will see more. A garden takes careful planning to think ahead of each stage."

"Forgive my ignorance," he laughed. "Do you actually believe something will grow from planting eggshells?"

"Oh, Doctor Watson, everything will. Eggshells are part of the magic. They feed the earth magnificently so it can produce what I expect from it."

He squatted. "If I read these packets correctly, you have planted quite a few flowers, as much or more than the hearty vegetables. Yet, I see no flowers in your home."

"Never pick a flower from a garden! They are the barriers that insects cannot penetrate. I cultivate marigolds first, to be the most protection for my young plants. You will see they are a formidable defender. Doctor, if you please?" He offered his hand, and I rose.

"Flowers, who would think they have a definite use beyond the gift of beauty?"

"And for the bees, gardens need bees to get along."

I rinsed my tools and hands at the rain barrel. "Doctor, you are welcome to join me when I begin my tilling."

"Yes, thank you, Mrs. Hudson, I would like that." [5]

Early Spring Garden Preparation

Shakespeare said it, "Proud-pied April, dressed in all his trim, hath put a spirit of youth in everything." We feel it, the rise of sap in the trees, as do the returning bees and birds. It's time to clean out winter's dust, get up from our cosy hearth and put our hands in the soil, and envision our new spring garden. [6]

1. A ball of twine. Two-foot-high bamboo or wood stakes.

2. Decide upon the outer dimensions of your garden and the beds you want. With your paths, be generous. I recommend 3-foot-width beds with 2 or 3-foot-wide paths around for ease of working.

3. Measure out as many as your garden and your helpers can support.

4. Stake out the corners of each bed and secure the twine from stake to stake. These are your beds. At this point, you can reassess the layout, walk the paths, and decide what changes are to be made.

5. The actual borders are created with stone, log, board, or short fencing. Lay them out along the twined boundary. Wooden boards need to be lowered into the ground by fifty per cent.

6. The paths may be planted with ground cover, yet will need to be scythed or mowed frequently and weeds pulled. They will lessen each year as the root takes them out.

7. Cover each bed with animal or fish manure. Best to do this late fall or early winter as manure needs time to mature.

8. And be sure to have it finished by March. Although setting up in early spring, just before planting, is acceptable in a pinch.

Vegetables And Their Complements

"I used to visit and revisit it a dozen times a day, and stand in deep contemplation over my vegetable progeny with a love that nobody could share or conceive of who had never taken part in the process of creation. It was one of the most bewitching sights in the world to observe a hill of beans thrusting aside the soil, or a row of early peas just peeping forth sufficiently to trace a line of delicate green." Nathaniel Hawthorne. [7]

Gardens do best planted with complementary vegetables and flowers. Marigolds and nasturtiums are especially good for keeping insects away. Plant them liberally throughout the growing beds.

Do not worry about giving up space for growing vegetables. These flowers pay their way by keeping your plants healthy and pest-free.

Preparation for multiple plantings is essential. Lettuce comes up and grows fast. What will you next plant in that bed? Vegetables have their own best timing. For example, spinach is an excellent bushy early crop. But as soon as the weather warms, it goes out like a candle—harvest as needed, like lettuce. The choices of what to plant at this time of year are unlimited.

Winter gardening lengthens the growing season. Fresh food from the garden year-round is another joy of gardening in our British climate. We can still grow lettuces like kale, spinach, chicory, cabbages, turnip, leek, Brussels sprouts, and beetroot in much of winter. Plant late in the year and harvest throughout the cold months.

An example of how these vegetables immensely benefit our lives: For the last two hundred years, cabbages and turnips have been cultivated for winter feeding of farm livestock. Because of this, we no longer need to create salt meat. Before this, scurvy and leprosy cases were frequent throughout the country, but thanks to the wonderful cabbage and turnip, those terrible diseases are no longer with us.

The English Cottage Vegetable Garden

Aristotle must have been a gardener, for he said, "In all things of nature there is something of the marvellous." And if he with his great mind could plant seeds, I think that Mr Holmes could too. I dearly wish I had the power to convince him it is a much better way to survive monotony than cocaine!

Our courtyard garden grows in Central London. The mature London Plane Tree stands proudly on the north side, growing beds on the south side. Eight beds laid out as three-foot width-wise, each cut into three lengthwise rows—three-foot-wide paths in between for working around. We do not have room for large rose bushes, yet our trellised roses bloom throughout the summer and into the holidays.

British soil is rich and fertile. Our ideal weather is a blessing for growing things and requires only slight augmentation. London reflects the country, and my additions are few. There is no need for chemical fertiliser.

The varying condition of our air adds a distinct impediment. A good clean wet fog feeds the garden, but our dun-colour yellow variety is not fit for flora or fauna.

What to use as garden amendment depends on what your town has available and what your soil requires. I find fertiliser from fish or seaweed to be best and easily gained from the Worshipful Company of Fishmongers. Animal manure is excellent when composted in the sun for two years or more. Most farms will allow you to cart it away, but our city streets' ever-burgeoning state allows for simple acquisition. A powerful combination results from mixing it with rough-milled alfalfa.

Recipe for Fish Fertiliser

Using a hand grinder. Grind up the fish waste: bones, intestines, liver, gallbladder, heart, fins, tail, scales, heads/gills, and skin. Liquify as much as possible and work into the soil. Also, add it to your compost and the garden this way. The Natives of the Americas bury chunks of fish at the roots of their plants.

Please be aware that the pungent odour of this potent fertiliser may attract animals. Well-mix as compost and till directly into the soil is the best approach for this. Plant it deeply or fence the garden appropriately.

Herb Garden

> "I plant rosemary all over the garden, so pleasant is it to know that at every few steps one may draw the kindly branchlets through one's hand, and have the enjoyment of their incomparable incense; and I grow it against walls, so that the sun may draw out its inexhaustible sweetness to greet me as I pass."
> Gertrude Jekyll. [8]

My herb garden lies beneath our London Plane Tree and along the outer edges of the garden. Blue periwinkles at the base of the tree mixed with lily of the valley. Further out where the shade is lighter, and along the sunny sides, we plant Chives, Thyme, Basil, Tarragon, Marjoram, Borage, Garlic, Garden

Cress, Mustard, Horseradish, Chervil, Angelica, Lemon Balm, Mint, Parsley, Rosemary, and Strawberry.

If you plant Lily of the Valley, teach your children they are deadly poisonous. And plant herbs at a safe distance and catnip elsewhere.

Be careful with mint and strawberry. They will take over the garden if not regularly pruned. Periwinkle will choke the Lily if not cut back. Its evergreen qualities are especially welcome after most of the garden is fallow and the planetree's hand-shaped leaves have fallen into our compost pile.

Plant rosemary throughout the garden and at the edges for its lavender-grey blooms and sweet scent. As the garden's early spring welcoming downbeat, this evergreen blooms before the return of any other scented flower in early spring.

Herb and Flower Pot-pourri Recipe

Gather rose petals and sweet geranium. Dry and pack into jars with bay salt and kitchen salt. Prepare Sweet Verbena, Lavender, Bay, and Rosemary the same way. Cover Orange peel strips with cloves. Combine in a large bowl adding equal amounts of Allspice, Clove, Mixed Spice, Mace, Gum Benzoin, Gum Storax or Styrax, and five times as much Atkinson's Violet powder. Mix the petals, leaves, and Orange well with spices and store them in glass jars for gifts.

The Rhythm of the Broadfork

In the early spring, nothing can convince me to break my back with a shovel or hoe to till the garden. How do I do so? The answer is the ease of working with a good broadfork in my planting rows. One stands on it in a much more appropriate upright posture and one's back is not taxed in the digging.

Our blacksmith forges the iron blades, metal crossbar, and solid wooden handles. His design makes assembly simple. Carriage bolts go into the slots and secure the ends of the Ash handles into sockets on the end of the crossbar.

The broadfork is a powerful and highly efficient tool. For centuries, gardeners have used it to loosen clay, rocky, and dry soils and prepare the ground for the addition of amendments. And for harvesting potatoes, carrots, and other root vegetables. One stands on four broad pickaxes, using weight and gravity to till instead of bending one's back and blistering one's hands.

Brute strength is unnecessary in broadforking. The movement is rhythmic, almost balletic. It is an enjoyable pastime, so in the end, it seems to have gone by too fast. Try that with a shovel!

Tomato the Fruit of Life

"Life is itself a school, and Nature always a fresh study," said Hugh Miller. Nature's changes can be surprising, some we once knew as vegetables are now considered fruits. [9]

The tomato underwent patient cultivation in the Americas for centuries before making its way to Italy, Spain, and France. Gradually herded by careful selection and keen observation into the varieties we enjoy.

Though in some countries, including ours, it was once deemed poisonous, so had to prove itself worthy.

All tomatoes require full sun and are best in well-draining soil. Adjust your watering schedule based on the weather. Water freely on dry days, and let it drain in wet.

Begin by cutting poles or bamboo to five- or six-foot height, enough for each plant. When the vines are tall enough, securely embed a pole for each, careful not to harm the roots.

Thus, begins the tying up of the tomatoes. Tomato vines will happily crawl along the ground like squash, but this only affords worms better access to the fruit. Instead, tie them up with long strips of soft cloth. It is a delicate process that requires some care as the vines break easily. I save shirts with lighter summer materials for each new season. You may tear long strips of at least one inch in width from the material. Wrap the cloth gently around the vine, crisscross the cloth loosely, and tie the material to the pole, not the vine. Take care not to pinch the vine when tying.

Following average growth, it is necessary to untie gently and then retie the vine higher on the bamboo. This fruit requires height and care to grow. The sweet scent of flowering and growing tomatoes and their anticipation makes tying the tomatoes my favourite part of gardening.

Practical Gardening

In the middle of June, when the garden is at its zenith, we might face a drought even in England. No rain for a month, and the ground is hard as iron. And from the east, the wind brings a green-fly devastation!

Each day tending an English Cottage garden is new. I skilfully plan it out, and yet the garden takes me along on its wonderfully improvised journey. We rejoice in the fact our backyard garden is steps away from clean flowing water. It takes time, muscle, and commitment to keep it from parching in such drastic weather.

Sometimes in gardening a drought, an early freeze, or an autumnal downpour, without good enough drainage or the beetles swarm in droves from above or below. The garden will not wait for our comprehension. The gardener must act or face losing all.

One just has to throw up one's hands for a moment, then pick up the pieces, and go on.

This was the time to consult the friends we made in gardening clubs or our University Agricultural Colleges and Extensions. Proven scientific advice for farmers and gardeners was an invaluable resource in times of crisis. Never fear to ask for help or to learn something new. The English Arts & Crafts Movement has added much to our libraries, supporting a science of farming and gardening available to anyone.

Helpful Friends

1. University Extension Programs and Master Gardeners.
2. Local Horticultural and Garden Societies.

3. British Beekeepers Association: Stoneleigh, Coventry

4. Cambridge Department of Agriculture.

5. The Royal Agricultural College: Cirencester, Gloucestershire.

6. The Bath and West of England Society and Southern Counties Association for the Encouragement of Agriculture, Arts, Manufactures, and Commerce: Bath.

The Glasshouse

Today Jack and his friends from the Baker Street Irregulars created a glasshouse in our garden out of old windows. Watching this handy young gentleman oversee the building of a home for our growing seedlings was instructive in the utter uniqueness of the human spirit. These street urchins rarely see a roof over their own heads. All the materials they used were scrounged from scrap.

The size is six-foot-high by four-foot-wide. A simple wooden frame holds the windows. The roof is made of glass. The windows cascade from the top to prevent water leakage. Flagstones for flooring. And anchored to the wall. On a worktable, they are happily planting seedlings. Doctor Watson and I are witnesses to the potential of these discarded children.

The Abundant Harvest

"In seed-time learn, in harvest teach, in winter enjoy."
William Blake. [10]

Our ancestors celebrated the harvest from the fall equinox to Michaelmas on the 29th of September. The large village festivals and feasts of old are stories of another time. Yet, we may still celebrate with a good goose supper and my Michaelmas Bannock cake. Here and there, harvest fetes still exist. Even in London, you may find my favourite, the Harvest Festival of the Sea in Spitalfields.

Harvesting is an ongoing event that follows nature's timing. Every harvest of every crop has its own welcome and its own duties. Some happily become the following week's meals, some are gifts, preserved appropriately, added to breads, cakes, pies, or are traded for the things we need. Be creative in your use of this abundance, and with lodgers also to feed, and our Irregular helpers, our kitchen bespeaks the joys of the harvest all year long.

Harvesting Seeds

As each crop reaches harvest, there is a further joy to be found in seed harvesting. Today's 19th-century gardener has access to a variety of seed catalogues. Yet, the seeds from our own produce can become the basis for the coming year's abundance. Flowers are effortless to harvest. Within the divine beauty of each flower is its own perpetuation. Allow the seeds to dry on the stalks or vines and simply catch them before they fall. Crush the pods between your fingers or keep the flower intact, dry and save it for the next planting.

Garner fruit or vegetable seeds from within the fruit before cooking. Clean off the pulp and air dry. Gather them into envelopes, label them, and keep them in a dry place, your earth or root cellar, near to where the herbs are hanging.

Strawberries, raspberries, and grapes are perennials and will continue to produce year in and year out. It is their nature to proliferate, and they require thinning out.

Raspberry canes can be especially worrisome and require pruning or training into the shape you require. Like rose bushes, they prove a compelling challenge as you mould them with good stout gloves. If you do not have the inclination to wrestle with this unruly fruit, I recommend keeping it out of your garden altogether.

Strawberries are prolific. Prune them to grow in the space allotted. These fruits require only sun and rain to produce a worthwhile crop.

I have never grown wine grapes, so I have nothing to say on the subject.

Thoughts on Chemical Amendments [12]

The recent turn towards chemical garden amendment in the gardening and farming community is one I staunchly find lacking, especially as the proven addition of fish manure to the garden or farm superbly enhances its growth. Possibly some research into making this more accessible would prove worthy, but I can see no need for chemical enhancement.

I would invite you to take care when considering using any of these products. Some are imported guano and can safely be used as augmentation. Now there are products that add to the guano substances created in a chemical laboratory. The promise of these chemicals is untested. Even Mr Holmes, who is a master chemist, questions their ease of use verses the potential for hidden problems. What does the future hold for our good English soil, its helpful insects, and birds once they are infiltrated by these untried chemicals? The price may be dear. It is yet to be determined and seems entirely unnecessary to me.

From our island, we have access to the best fertiliser ever created, the fish of the rivers, lakes, and seas. This adds to the soil only that which is natural to our diet and adds healthy material to our gardens.

As our world approaches the changes of the new century, we have as a people discovered the creation and sale of new products that later prove as false as Gripe Water. Or as harmful as cocaine. How many of us got involved with that manufactured evil because the medical profession touted it as the latest in chemical wonders? I believe science's novel approach to soil augmentation may hold similar disadvantages for the future of our country.

Sherlock Holmes by Frederic Dorr Steele and Sidney Paget [1]

A TOAST DARLING

A tribute in one act.

CAST OF CHARACTERS

SHERLOCK HOLMES. The Great Detective.

JEREMY BRETT. Shakespearian actor and portrayer of SHERLOCK HOLMES.

HERALD/EDWARD HARDWICKE/DOCTOR WATSON. Soldier, doctor, MR HOLMES'S biographer.

WOMAN IN BLUE TROUSERS

REPROBATE

PUB DWELLERS

PLACE

Prince Albert Pub in Battersea, London, UK.

TIME

Present day.

ACT I, SCENE I

SETTING

A traditionally comfortable Public House in residential South London. Smokers cordially gather at tables under a large, welcoming cafe awning. It is raining, of a variety that farmers crave, and Londoners barely acknowledge. Cabs splash through puddles as they approach the bridge.

AT RISE

SHERLOCK HOLMES, in black frockcoat and topper, is smoking at an outside table, carefully observing 21st Century Londoners.

HERALD

"Once upon a time in London, SHERLOCK HOLMES met with the actor, JEREMY BRETT. A bottle of champagne under his arm, he stepped out to the pavement for a smoke but found he left his cigarettes behind."

SHERLOCK HOLMES

(Rises and shakes JEREMY'S hand like a brother and offers his silver cigarette case.)

"Thank you for coming."

"Help yourself. It has probably been a while."

JEREMY

(Dressed in a navy blue jumper, white trousers and trainers, red socks. Lights cigarette, enjoys the taste.)

"It is the tobacco, which I find most irksome."

SHERLOCK HOLMES

(Smiles.)

"All right, you are entitled."

JEREMY

"Ha! No deerstalker, no meerschaum pipe! I thought as much."

SHERLOCK HOLMES

"It was that illustrator, Paget and that American, Steele. Even if one never read a word of Doyle's stories, their images were so proliferated. But who would wear a hunting cap in the capital city of London?"

JEREMY

"Exactly! You really are paying attention."

(Pops the cork, fills their glasses, hands one to SHERLOCK, and clinks the detective's glass.)

"They can pull a fine pint here but know nothing of champagne. I thought, a toast, darling. To friendship!"

SHERLOCK HOLMES

(Raises his glass.)

"And genius! MR BRETT, I must commence these proceedings by thanking you for *The Secret of Sherlock Holmes*! At that time in your career, you could have initiated anything: played the lead in a Hollywood film, rested in the Bahamas, filmed your *Tempest*, founded your own theatre, school, or, like Rathbone, written your autobiography. Whatever your heart desired. Instead, for my keenest pleasure, you took it upon yourself to conceive, write, produce, and star in that gorgeous West End play. It was a supremely generous one-hundredth birthday tribute!"

HERALD

"The actor observed the man he once thought of as a black beetle, a damaged penguin. In his top hat and knee-length skirts, he made the outmoded frock-coat look good."

JEREMY

"Of course, darling! Why not?"

"The timing was everything. My company was absolutely superb. Only TED HARDWICKE was a little hesitant. He needed a break and possibly thought I did, too. If we presented it in New York, we would have swept the Tonys that year."

(He watches HOLMES as his attention shifts to the last table.)

"How are you, sir?"

SHERLOCK HOLMES

"Do you see that young WOMAN IN THE BLUE TROUSERS? She is in for a pernicious time, flirting with that REPROBATE."

(He quickly rises to his feet.)

"Excuse me…"

JEREMY

(Grabs HOLMES'S arm.)

"MR HOLMES, please reel in your chivalrous desires. Here, that would lead to a brawl. I'll back you up if you must. I've had my nose broken before."

SHERLOCK HOLMES

"As have I."

(They study each other's faces for a moment. Then sit.)

"Even though some exercise would be welcome, I believe you are correct. The ability to observe as I do can sometimes foster unwarranted consequences."

"I understand apologies are in order. I missed your previous invitation for tea at the Savoy."

JEREMY

(Laughs.)

"Well, we both did."

SHERLOCK HOLMES

(Pats JEREMY'S back.)

"I should have been more careful with you."

"It would be exceptional to see your portrayal at 65, 75, 85…"

JEREMY

(Blanches at the thought of playing the same role for 30 years!)

"How did William Gillette do it? Forgive me, but Doyle is harder to play than any of Shakespeare's characters."

SHERLOCK HOLMES

"Gillette did not subsume himself in the role as completely nor as recklessly as you did, MR BRETT. There was a lot of William Gillette in his interpretation. Have you seen what is out there now?"

(HOLMES slowly shakes his head.)

"Some of the new writers have it right and I am doing my best to inspire them. Yet too many prefer to project their fantasies onto me rather than concoct a good mystery. An affair with a 15-year-old girl? A sociopath! Me? Even WATSON would steer clear of such sensationalism. My life, my science, and my honour are dedicated to a merciful justice! How can one write one word without doing the research? It is appalling. Moriarty! The Ripper! They were sociopaths. One would have to be to carry out their evil deeds. I am a shining knight of truth and justice!"

"Not one of them understands my feelings for *the* woman. Least of all, WATSON!"

JEREMY

"Run, my dear, from anything that may not strengthen your precious, budding wings. Run like hell my dear, from anyone likely to put a sharp knife into the sacred, tender vision of your beautiful heart." [3]

SHERLOCK HOLMES

(Smiles.)

"Ah, Hafiz's poetry was very handy in 'A Case of Identity.'"

JEREMY

"That poor girl is probably still pining for her Hosmer Angel."

SHERLOCK HOLMES

(Laughing.)

"I will let you in on a secret. WATSON didn't always write them up precisely as they transpired. I did inform her of the truth. She left home over it and set up a prosperous business in Leadenhall Street. WATSON makes good use of her typing service and we are regularly invited to tea. But the Doctor felt his version was more dramatic."

(Shrugs. Lights a cigarette.)

"My boy, your spectacular performance changed everything, yet was unreachable for most. No one was as willing as you were to pour their life energy into the work. But we both know it was the way. No one revelled in smoking my pipe like you did. Some said your acting was so real it was unsettling."

"Thank you for that, MR BRETT. You carved out my dangerous reality with your breath, your dancer's movements, and your mighty battles to present WATSON'S stories word-for-word on film. I am grateful for every one of those fights. WATSON said it in *The Valley of Fear*, 'Mediocrity knows nothing higher than itself, but talent instantly recognises genius."

JEREMY

(Douses his cigarette.)

"If there's one thing I learned by attempting to portray you for so long, it was that you were the genius, darling. Please call me JEREMY."

SHERLOCK HOLMES

"Who does or does not display genius. That is not our purview. We act. Not judge. I know, I have let a few malefactors go. But that is not justice, it is sentiment."

"It was your imaginative leap that Doyle had given me a modicum of the softer feelings. You played upon them like my Stradivarius. There was genius in that. Especially in your unveiling of the blood moving beneath what Doyle thought was impenetrable granite. And your humour, thank you for that. MR HARDWICKE called it a whiff of Edwardian acting."

JEREMY

(Smiles at the mention of his dear friend.)

"Bless your darling heart, MR HOLMES. I had my time, and it was a wild ride. At the start, I couldn't fathom how to find your parameters—thankfully, I stopped running from the darkness around you and realised you also hated it."

(Lights a cigarette as the rain begins in earnest. He gestures to HOLMES, and they move back from the puddles that threaten a soaking with each passing cab.)

"All my troubles with the character changed with the children who came to see *The Secret of Sherlock Holmes*. At the conclusion, still dressed as you, darling, I sat at the edge of the stage and conversed with the three, four, and five-year-olds in

138

the audience. They gave me what no one else could. Their belief in you—and me as you. They knew well of the darkness of dreams. That you dedicated your life and mighty gifts to the extinction of that darkness. They knew you were succeeding."

"To the children, we were heroes. They trusted me with their nightmares. It was through their eyes that I saw your sword of justice cut between darkness and light. I love people and saw how in your own way, you sir, did, too."

SHERLOCK HOLMES

"JEREMY, I am sorry for the confusion, but it was your confusion. How can one consider that a mind like mine could be empty of emotion?"

"Certainly you were aware that in my trade there were times when acting skills proved necessary? I confess, that for me, this was one of its allures. But a stern face was more my emulation of Sir Henry Irving than WATSON'S misunderstanding of the Indigenous American Indian."

"You, my boy, were too impressed by other portrayals. The usual choice was to play that imperious yet unemotional man. Which, as you know, was impossible to sustain and not how the stories were written—most of all, not me! Even Irving was criticised for his diction, mannerisms, and literary scholarship. Jeremy, you had one up on him there."

"Doyle was also foiled by this. He never accepted that I was my own man. No, he battled for control of what he thought was his Frankenstein until the end of his days. And then his family took it on. 'Grit in a sensitive instrument, or a crack in one of his own high-power lenses, would not be more

139

disturbing than a strong emotion in a nature such as his. Poppycock!'"

(Grinds out his fag.)

"Just what is it about genius that people fear? WATSON, too, sometimes went overboard in defining an aspect of my personality, but I surmise the total was hard to make comprehensible. Ha! Now, the latest bull is to psychoanalyse me and attach the day's most popular diagnosis. It makes me want to wretch!"

(Lights another cigarette for JEREMY and one for himself. They create a fog under the awning.)

"But you got past that dear boy, you found me, you alone saw the dichotomy. You saw the mind and the man, as WATSON truly does."

JEREMY

"You know, dear heart, I really am more of a WATSON."

(Savours his champagne and refills their glasses.)

SHERLOCK HOLMES

"Your ability at deflection is another likeness between us and combined with your sleight of hand requires intelligence to envision your footsteps walking on tiptoe and backwards in the dust. JEREMY, you are wiser than WATSON. And definitely more so than that American gunslinger for whom you portrayed WATSON."

(Pats JEREMY on the back.)

"And you could be my twin. You are as athletic. We come from the same country squire background. Share Huguenot ancestry, grew up as neighbours, are both youngest sons, and have an older brother with art in our blood. We have both enriched our lives by practising the gifts of the East. We chose our own professions and went at them with the same brilliant ferocity and became recognised masters. To be without work affects us equally, yes?"

JEREMY

(Nods his approval.)

"However, darling, I prefer champagne with friends to cocaine injections."

SHERLOCK HOLMES

"Nevertheless, you have said you don't think like me, nor use my methods to solve problems, and no one is as sagacious as I am. But JEREMY, my boy, that was your means of keeping the public at bay. You were rather protective of your private life, an intelligent way to be in your profession. I watched your masterful interpretation of my world with exquisite joy. But my dear, JEREMY, dyslexia does not affect intelligence, and I wager yours is considerable."

JEREMY

"My blushes, SHERLOCK. I will accept it from you. I had learned to present my humble side to survive in a world where a boy with some advantages is brutally cut down to size. Silly, really, since we are all the same size. There is no need."

(Lights another cigarette.)

"A man with gentle sensibilities quickly learned to denigrate himself publicly. It is sad to be forced into playing this one-up, one-down role. I see so many children's futures chipped away while their self-esteem bleeds out in the backyards and the schoolrooms."

(JEREMY turns and faces SHERLOCK.)

"But your reaching hand to the children who never even had the luxury of school is famous. Why, one of your longest-running fan clubs is named after them."

SHERLOCK HOLMES

(Sighs.)

"JEREMY, my province is to plant seeds, not till or harvest. And I'm sorry, my boy, there were times during that forced Manchester solitude when I couldn't believe your pleadings."

(Nods apologetically.)

"Not that they weren't heartfelt, my dear boy."

JEREMY

(Leaps onto a chair, as if it were a stage.)

"O for a Muse of fire, that would ascend the brightest heaven of invention, a kingdom for a stage, princes to act, and monarchs to behold the swelling scene!" [6]

"You couldn't believe ME?"

(The smokers applaud. JEREMY half bows and jumps down.)

SHERLOCK HOLMES

(Stands next to JEREMY.)

"Thank you, JEREMY. Eye to eye we are the same height, with dark colouring, and slight build. Yet, we both know there is whipcord beneath."

(He waves them to their seats.)

"JEREMY, you worked without sleep or nourishing food. Yet, not like me. Therefore, it hurt you, in ways it rarely did me. For a meal or two on a case, I sharpened my faculties this way. I do know how ruinous such a way of living can be. But yours was continuous. And it destroyed your handsome body. Living that way could ruin anyone's mind, JEREMY. There were times when you acted and thought like an angel. Yet the human form was not that strong."

"Like MR HARDWICKE, I was there with you to the end. I revelled in your Shakespearian voice and brilliant actor's choices, how you translated my movements into graceful acrobatics. I climbed up that fireplace, threw down onto so many floors with you, leapt over that settee like an Olympic medallist, and beat Lestrade again and again. My eyebrow rose with yours. I raced up all those stairs and across those green lawns with you. I basked in Irene's beauty and her exceptional voice, and wore her token always. Triumphantly returned from three years of travel as the explorer, Sigerson, from places no Englishman could go. I watched as your perfect and subtle comedic senses broadened my horizons!"

JEREMY

(Nonchalantly lights a cigarette.)

"That's lovely, darling. Thank you, SHERLOCK. I'm touched. I never knew you could be so forthcoming."

SHERLOCK HOLMES

(With a twinkle in his eye.)

"JEREMY, like the prayer you carried in your pocket. For those ten years, they were my footprints in the sand. All the work you brought to it, the devotion and joy and clarity you contributed. Your acting style—it is not only that I inspired you—you truly became me and, what is more, for those ten years, I was you!"

"Your meditative listening, your hatred of class distinctions, and your friendship with that fixed point in a changing age, so like mine. Then you moved into realms no one had before. Your fearless portrayal of the pleasure I derived from cocaine, and most daring of all, how it sickened me and my final renouncement. You saw me as I am, JEREMY, a unique, intelligent, and sensitive gentleman. A genius—not a freak! Not some costume, speaking perfect Victorian English. A name ripped out of the pages of a book! Though you didn't plan it this way, you used the last years of your life to study me and grant me life. Your generosity was legendary, but none could imagine the power of this 'souvenir of gratitude' to me, my friend. [7] When viewers watch these films, they don't only see JEREMY BRETT. They see me! Thank you."

(SHERLOCK doffs his topper, bows theatrically to JEREMY.)

JEREMY

(Blushes and brings him back to the table. Toasts.)

144

"SHERLOCK HOLMES, may you always dwell in infinite possibility."

"Of course, darling, you are deliciously incorrigible. I confess I did enjoy your touch of the dramatic, not suffering fools, sending people off, turning my back on the PM, not bowing to the King, not said 'sorry' or 'goodnight' or 'thank you', and expressing your outrageous and very pointed anger!"

(Puts out his cigarette.)

"It is true, as you say, give me work, and I am in my own proper atmosphere. There is so much to share, to teach, and to be taught. We humans are so flawed and yet so beautiful, and both realisations are necessary."

SHERLOCK HOLMES

(HOLMES listens intently with eyes closed.)

JEREMY

"I learned to separate from the dark times in my life and the darkness I thought I saw in you. You will always speak to me through Doyle's words."

(Lights another cigarette, and enjoys its flavour.)

"But if I may ask, MR HOLMES, are you angelic?"

SHERLOCK HOLMES

(Laughs. With one quick swing of his walking stick, he pushes on the bulging awning, releasing a splash of rainwater over JEREMY, the cafe tables, and the smokers.)

REPROBATE and SMOKING PATRONS

"Hey, mate!"

(REPROBATE rises menacingly to his feet. GIRL IN BLUE TROUSERS takes his arm and persuades him to sit.)

SHERLOCK HOLMES

(Laughs.)

"A fine baptismal, don't you think? Surely JEREMY, you know, I am a Muse. More cunning than angels and not any more holy than you are. Nor do we live or die. There's a lot of freedom in that. But you, I think, have more than a touch of the angelic in you."

(Lights a cigarette.)

JEREMY

"How does one become a Muse? Have you always been such?"

SHERLOCK HOLMES

"I can't enlighten you on that point. I just am."

(Smokes.)

"Conan Doyle was a visionary with the ability to reach beyond the realms of his earthly existence. The game was splendid at first."

JEREMY

"It took me quite a while to give in to your prodding. I was afraid of where you'd lead me, and what happened to other actors who took you on. How I would ultimately fare next to them. None of this detained me. To me, fear is the bugle that begins the race. But darling, you are formidable."

SHERLOCK HOLMES

"Bah! Blame is just a waste of life, JEREMY. I too run at that self-same horn. You speak of a character beloved by the world."

"First—I am alive!"

"Second—The world watched you become me for ten exquisite years, on stage, and through all forty-one films. As you did in *The Hound,* you used your fear, loneliness, and grief to portray me as a man of compassion."

(Lights a cigarette.)

"Yet at the end, when illness cut you down, you made the most courageous choices an actor could make—to show them all, as expressed by me, the crumbling edifice, and then to 'die' on screen. Every actor says they want that, but you shared it with us as your parting gift! Your portrayal was so real it was as unsettling as life. Not as Doyle envisioned, the ageing beekeeping recluse pottering his last years away in the Sussex Downs. As if I would discard my life in London as easily as this cigarette. You put my demise centre stage at No. 221B Baker Street! I am immensely grateful for that, JEREMY."

JEREMY

"I was sure you would understand. In those films, I had the most perfect chance to show your genuine friendship with WATSON, and my best friend, Ted, made that easy. When I saw your possibilities, my palette expanded. I freely used your humour, and how you really loved and needed fallible ole darling, WATSON. I wanted to show that close relationship which is so missed by men today. The camaraderie of boys on an adventure, that's sadly castaway for the responsibilities of manhood. The excitement of the hunt and the joy of solving the puzzle, even though it inevitably led to frustration, before beginning once again."

(His fingers hold a cigarette pointing at HOLMES.)

"Your loneliness and your need to be alone, your ability to see everything before anyone else."

(Looks to the last table and back to SHERLOCK.)

"Your intense love of and pursuit of true justice, no matter the cost to yourself. Your sense of fairness, and your deeply human capacity to forgive. Your ability to enlighten those around you, and even though you do not suffer fools, you took pity on some of them. I used all of it. I buttoned it on with your waistcoat."

SHERLOCK HOLMES

(Speaks through a thoughtful exhale of cigarette smoke.)

"It fit you exceedingly well. I think it is important at this point to establish just how a Muse works."

(Looks across to Battersea Park in an unfocused way and then to JEREMY.)

148

"When your first marvellous WATSON, David Burke, left after the 'Final Problem' film, it so happened that his wife, Anna Calder-Marshall, was working on a radio play of Titus Andronicus with EDWARD HARDWICKE. In her kindness, she searched for some way to help you with your predicament."

"So, I mentioned to her lovely and open mind (actors are so sensitive to the Muse) that EDWARD HARDWICKE and DOCTOR WATSON shared the same birthdate. She, of course, graciously carried it through."

JEREMY

"A thousand blessings for that. It was the greatest act of compassion!"

(Pulls HOLMES to his feet, and hugs him in an all-encompassing way. HOLMES reciprocates in kind.)

REPROBATE

(Yells.)

"Hey, keep it to yourselves, mates! This is the Prince Albert, not the King's Arms!"

SHERLOCK HOLMES

(Laughs at the REPROBATE.)

"Your conversation is most entertaining. Pray, take your seat and try not to confound it with your head!"

(HOLMES watches the REPROBATE sit back down. Then gestures JEREMY and himself into their chairs.)

149

JEREMY

(Laughs and continues past the interruption.)

"David and my odd couple pairing had constructed a solid foundation during the one and a half years and thirteen films we played HOLMES and WATSON. Together we had built the edifice that was soon to be Granada's number one series. I know I was extremely lucky to have two such exceptional actors by my side."

"My dear TED, was a best friend to me. You know, he grew up in Hollywood. Nigel Bruce was playing WATSON when TED was a boy, and he befriended HARDWICKE. During our days at Granada, Bruce's portrayal was criticised. We all agreed that WATSON should be the soldier, the doctor, the friend—not the buffoon. TED, dear heart, defended Bruce against the throng and helped us to see how important comedy was during wartime. TED was a true gentleman and a great, great friend."

SHERLOCK HOLMES

"Well, let's not quibble about WATSON."

(Smiles.)

"You are a supremely talented, kind-hearted, and brave soul, JEREMY. It is a courageous way to live in this world. An English gentleman at a time when almost no one is, both you and MR HARDWICKE set the bar high in that regard. Thank you for that. Do you yet see how like me you are?"

(Lights a cigarette.)

JEREMY

"Yes, it took me some time to uncover. But I always celebrate life, like to play, and tell jokes, even though I sometimes forget the punchline. TED thought that endearing. One thing I happily uncovered in my research was that you also had a sense of humour and seriously enjoy playing tricks. I have and am a good friend, was married to the most marvellous, gutsy, intelligent, beautiful, and giving woman on the planet. I have the most brilliant children. They are my legacy. Even after all these years, I still have avid fans."

(Lights a cigarette.)

"Of course, darling, no one can match you for that."

SHERLOCK HOLMES

"JEREMY, did you read, *A Study in Scarlet?* Keeping potential lovers at arm's length was an absolute imperative. My new profession was exhilarating, the possibilities, and the connections building from the study I had taken on. My own little practice was showing promise. With application my powers increased, my intuition quickened, and I was unmistakably certain this was my correct path. Each day brought new discoveries and excitement. No time for the entanglements of my peers. I was a student of the world and couldn't get enough. Does this not sound like your time at the National Theatre?"

JEREMY

"Jonathan Swift said, 'The best doctors in the world are Doctor Diet, Doctor Quiet, and Doctor Merryman.' [9] I added 'Doctor

Theatre' to the mix. He got me through the exhaustion of those absolutely marvellous days."

SHERLOCK HOLMES

"Yes, well, we were both younger men."

(Glances to the last table. Holds out his hand, they shake.)

"JEREMY, if you need me, I will not be difficult to find. A parting toast: 'Impossible is not a fact. It's an opinion.'" [10]

WOMAN IN BLUE TROUSERS

(The WOMAN IN BLUE TROUSERS jumps up and punches the REPROBATE with a hard left to the chin and leaves.)

SHERLOCK HOLMES

(Wearing a cat that ate the canary smile.)

"Women are never to be entirely trusted."

JEREMY

(Smiles, they shake hands.)

"Farewell, dear heart, thank you for answering my invitation and for your kind words. Let's keep the joke going that neither showed up."

SHERLOCK HOLMES

(Touches his topper, steps into a black carriage which appears out of nowhere, climbs in, and sits next to WATSON.)

WATSON

"Where to, HOLMES?"

SHERLOCK HOLMES

(Knocks on the roof of the hansom.)

"Baker Street, Cabbie, as fast as you can!"

HERALD

"The horses fly across the river. The jingle of their harness and the rhythm of their hooves echo in the streets. Up through Chelsea and the West End, to disappear where Regent's Park touches Baker Street."

CHANGE OF SCENE

ACT I, SCENE 2

PLACE: Wyndham's Theatre, London. *The Secret of Sherlock Holmes* play starring JEREMY BRETT and EDWARD HARDWICKE. [9]

TIME: 1989.

JEREMY BRETT

(Costumed like SHERLOCK HOLMES, in black frock-coat and topper. JEREMY bows from the stage. Then encourages the children to join him.)

HERALD

"The children rushed down the aisles, clambered into the front rows. They brought their drawings and their books. JEREMY sat cross-legged at the apron edge of the stage. For a golden hour, JEREMY BRETT listened to their stories of how SHERLOCK HOLMES, like a knight of old, slew the dragons that visited them in nightmares. The actor then addressed their questions as faithfully as would HOLMES."

CURTAIN

Frederic Dorr Steele, Sherlock Holmes in disguise. [1]

Crime is common. Humour is rare.

The Many Deaths of Sherlock Holmes – A Parody

"Well, really!' he cried, and then he choked; and laughed again until he was obliged to lie back, limp and helpless, in the chair." A Scandal in Bohemia.

On a gorgeous spring morning, our windows were opened to the intoxicating perfume wafting in from the park. We had finished one of Mrs Hudson's best breakfasts, and Holmes was lighting his first pipe of the day. I was at my desk, putting the finishing touches on our latest adventure for *The Strand Magazine*.

Holmes was now leaning out my window, eager as a retriever in his attempts to pull me from my work for a walk in the park.

"Watson, a better view of the emerging beauty of Regent's Park is achieved this way."

I turned, and in the tight space inadvertently knocked into him.

"Wat-son!" he said with consternation and disappeared through the window.

Alarmed, I rushed down the stairs, following his descent and out to the pavement, but he wasn't there. With both arms waving above his head, he shouted from the park entrance across the street, "Hello! Watson!"

"Lord Harry, fooled again! I swear that man must have bounced."

Even without my hat or stick, I, of course, joined him for a spring ramble. His excited voice, much louder than I would have liked, filled me in on the science behind Hofmeister's proof of the sexual life of plants as their purpose in nature and of each tree's beflowered attainments.

Following the cases I entitled, "The Disappearance of Lady Francis Carfax," and "The Adventure of the Three Gables," there was a dearth of unusual or unsolved cases. Nothing for Holmes to sink his teeth into. My worst fears unfolded when Holmes had time on his hands. I was grateful to find his cocaine bottle still gathering dust on the shelf. Yet where his brilliant imagination led him took all of my deductive abilities.

My research of his desk and the newspapers he dropped to the carpet led me on a wild goose chase across the Thames to Wandsworth, where I raced through the Gothic arches of St. Mary's Cemetery. There I found a simple casket about to be lowered six-feet underground.

"A sovereign to each of you if the lid comes off in a minute!" I demanded.

Breathing deeply, Holmes burst out of the box, sitting up in the casket as soon as the top was released. My friend was being buried alive! Whatever fiend had visited this on Sherlock Holmes would now have to answer to me.

Sherlock was chagrined at losing this chance to follow in Houdini's footsteps. He straddled the wooden coffin and angrily addressed the cemetery workers. "What is this? What do you think you are doing? Would you treat the great John Nevil Maskelyne this way? Put me back!"

The men withdrew in horror from the angry and very alive cadaver.

"Watson, this is your doing!"

He held out his hand. I took it and pulled him out of the horrible coffin.

"My dear Watson, I congratulate you for your accurate following of the clues. You really are progressing nicely."

Filled with anger and worry, I let him have it, "Like your insane flirtation with addictive drugs, cocaine, morphia, poppy, this relationship with Houdini is dangerous for you, Holmes. After all, he stands at five-foot-five inches and is supremely suited to his trade. Even I could observe that at over six-feet high you are most definitely unsuited to it. Where Houdini could freely move around in that accursed box, surely bending your knees just to fit it considerably restricts any chance of success. Heavens, Holmes, Houdini almost suffocated doing this trick! As your friend and physician, I strongly recommend you put an end to this magical infatuation and return to your detective practice. Immediately!"

"Your observations and speed are improving, Watson. For that, I am grateful. But surely you yourself must know that no man would take up my profession if it were not that danger attracts him."

The following day, the rain continued to beat and the autumn winds to rattle our windows. I was called out to identify a dead body discovered by a plate-layer named Mason, just outside Aldgate Station, on the London underground system.

"It was Sherlock Holmes,' he said. 'Fell off the roof of a first-class train carriage. There was no blood."

But on further inspection, it proved to be only a dummy filled with sand.

As I hung my soaking wet ulster and hat next to his perfectly dry topper, Holmes informed me,

"Watson, I devised the test to verify if a body could remain on the roof of an underground railway carriage while journeying from the back-stair windows of 13 Caulfield Gardens. To disembark at the point where the train emerges from the tunnel immediately before Aldgate Station."

At the time of the case, Holmes's alert mind had connected his finding of the points and the curve in the line. This single association led him to hypothesise the cause and type of death visited upon Cadogan West. All the interviews we carried out afterwards gave him the proof.

"Lost my old coat in that one, Watson. A test I could not complete at the time of the submarine case as my deductions and subsequent advertisement in the *Daily Chronicle* sped the matter to its successful conclusion. Not that brother Mycroft was at all bothered, he was happy with things as they were."

"But Holmes, why did the plate-layer brand the dummy as Sherlock Holmes?"

He laughed, "Oh, I attached my old deerstalker with a sturdy hatpin. You know how much I enjoy a bit of levity, old boy!"

He stoked our fire to its highest flashing.

"Come, Watson, draw your chair up, and warm your old bones, for the only problem which we have still to solve is how to while away these bleak autumnal evenings."

Another grey day dawned, full of rain. We were warming at the fire drinking hot coffee. Mrs Hudson had delivered a fresh pot and cleared our breakfast trays. A growler pulled up to the kerb and Holmes went to the window.

I said, "Who would be out on such a day? I hope they are not expecting us to become involved. The rain is coming down in sheets!"

"It's Lestrade. And very wet he is indeed," said, Holmes.

Inspector Lestrade ran up the stairs to our flat as Holmes crossed to unlock the door. The little professional was obviously in a hurry because his gun was drawn. His wet boots slid on the polished wood floor. Mrs Hudson had rolled up her hallway carpets for washing that day. At the door, he tripped and shot Holmes in the face.

Together we carried him to his bed, while I antiseptically staunched the bleeding and bandaged him. A shot of morphine to help him sleep, and Lestrade and I retired to the fire.

"How is he Doctor?"

Dazed, I said, "If he survives, he will be deformed for life."

I then focused my anger and unbelief on Lestrade.

"Why were you running with your gun in hand? What is the matter with you, Inspector? Gun safety is the first thing one learns!"

In a frenzy of terror at what he'd done, he feebly said, "I had only one bullet left and was reloading in the carriage. Thought I'd finish here where it's dry..." his voice trailed off.

"Well, Lestrade, you've certainly finished Holmes."

Filled with disgust at Lestrade's foibles, I left him and went to the bedroom to check on Holmes. His bed linen was soaked red with blood. Mrs Hudson would turn as livid when she saw it. But Holmes was missing.

Following a trail of blood, I found he had gone out his hallway door and down to the kitchen. Where I found him and Mrs Hudson sitting at the big wooden table sipping tea. Holmes had nary a scratch on him.

"There is no mystery, Watson. The bullet whizzed past my ear. Typical of Lestrade, he missed. It's probably lodged in the wall between the two photos of rushing streams. He may even have added a bullet pock to my rendition of VR. Oh, and thank you for the injection, my grey day is more rosy because of it," he laughed.

Mrs Hudson said, "Sit, Doctor, and have a cuppa. It will restore you."

"I don't know what's going on, but the mess Holmes left in his bedroom will undoubtedly upset your day, Mrs Hudson."

"You see, but you do not observe, Doctor!"

Holmes jumped up and steered me into the chair he had just vacated.

"Look again, my dear Watson. It is something new my friend Houdini invented, red disappearing blood. A most astute concoction! I'm testing it out, my boy, and your reaction is instructive. Do you perceive any red upon me? What's left will simply wash out in the laundry, Mrs Hudson."

"A fine test, Holmes. You will be the death of me yet!"

"No doubt, Watson, you were ascribing to me the Baron Gruner's villainous fate. I didn't expect to so comprehensively fool a man of medicine. Houdini shall be excited to learn of your involvement."

"Be sure to enlighten him about my supreme worry over your health as one of the factors in your experiment!"

"Forgive me, Watson, I owe you a thousand apologies. I never considered for a moment that you would be so taken in."

The following day was grey with a further threat of rain. With my pistol in my pocket, once more I was searching for Holmes. He left our lodgings early last night, costumed as a beggar. The Baker Street Irregulars spotted him among the dregs of the docks, in the vile alleys of Upper Swandam Lane. Between a slop shop and a gin shop, Inspector Bradstreet and I charged into the 'Bar of Gold' opium den. There we found the Lasker manager in an empty upstairs room. The mighty Bradstreet, fuelled by his sense of honour, grabbed the little man by the collar.

"Police brutality! Let go, I'll contact my solicitor!"

"A boatman on the River Thames spied a body being pushed out of this window. Heard the splash. Was he weighed down and taken out with the tide? Do you have any idea who you've murdered, my man?"

"A beggar is nobody!"

"The window is still open!" I said, "There's blood on the sill, Inspector!"

Bradstreet dropped the sailor into the custody of the bobbie at the door. Next, he joined me at the window. The tide was out and so were the mud-larks. Though humid, the rain had held, so we descended to the dark, oily, rusty bank. What we found was partially buried in the wet sand – a tattered old suit. One that I recognised.

"Inspector, this is Holmes's, without a doubt! It's one of his surveillance costumes."

"I'm glad the Yard doesn't expect us to wear such smelly disguises!"

"Beggars are invisible, Inspector. Sherlock blamed my stories for making this style of dress necessary to his practice. Now, I wish I'd never written a word! Oh, Holmes!" I wailed.

"We can't drag the Thames, Doctor. We'll have to wait and see if he pops up with the usual corpses."

"Inspector, your professional lack of empathy is unwarranted here. We are discussing the unthinkable! The untimely death of Sherlock Holmes," I said reverentially.

He patted my back. "Forgive me, Doctor Watson."

I pointed out to the river. "What is that?"

Behind a fast-moving river-steamer, was a tall, thin man in skivvies seemingly standing on the surface of the river. He had a rope in his hands, his feet were attached to Alpine skis, and Sherlock Holmes was waving at us. He looked so ridiculous. I had to laugh.

As he passed us by, I heard him call.

"You see, but you do not observe!"

Martin Van Maële illustration of Irene Adler for "A Scandal in Bohemia."

A Scandal in Baker Street

"And that was how a great scandal threatened to affect the kingdom of Bohemia, and how the best plans of Mr Sherlock Holmes were beaten by a woman's wit. He used to make merry over the cleverness of women, but I have not heard him do it of late. And when he speaks of Irene Adler, or when he refers to her photograph, it is always under the honourable title of *the* woman." [2]

This essay/story begins with the ending paragraph of Sir Arthur Conan Doyle's, "A Scandal in Bohemia." A splendid conclusion for a grand short story. One that has been the subject of much Sherlockian and Holmesian discussion. On this point Sherlockian.net confirms that Irene Adler's character is, "so compelling that she pervades our image of Sherlock Holmes forever after." [3]

Who was *the* woman to Sherlock Holmes?

Some who study Conan Doyle's work conjecture that he based his characterisation of Irene Adler on Lillie Langtry, the celebrated beauty, actress, mistress and friend of the Prince of Wales. Her beauty was so lauded that Oscar Wilde intoned, "I would rather have discovered Lillie Langtry than America."

Three Islamic women fighting the age-old battle for women's right to education in Indonesia, describe Irene Adler as, "strong-willed, assertive, independent, freedom of expression, self-confidence, strategic intelligence, and with the ability to challenge and change stereotypes and male views of women." [4]

As Conan Doyle put it, "She has the face of the most beautiful of women, and the mind of the most resolute of men." It is apparent that his character of Irene Adler moves readers in similar ways.

A brief plot summary of "A Scandal in Bohemia" follows:

The King of Bohemia involved Mr Sherlock Holmes in retrieving a compromising photograph from Miss Irene Adler, a contralto diva of the international opera circuit. The King was afraid Miss Adler would use this photograph to threaten his upcoming marriage to a Scandinavian Princess. During Holmes's surveillance of Adler's villa, he was caught up in her secret wedding to Godfrey Norton.

That very day, Sherlock hired all the out-of-work actors in London to create a scene in Serpentine Muse. Disguised as a clergyman, he gained entrance to her home, while Watson simulated a fire with a smoke rocket. Holmes knew that if Madam Adler-Norton believed her house was afire, she would reveal where the photograph was hidden. But she outsmarted him, escaped, and left a different photograph, and an explanatory letter for him to find in her safe instead. Holmes began the case by underestimating *the* woman and found in the end that it was he who was changed by this association.

A clue to Sherlock's unrequited feelings are mentioned in "The Boscombe Valley Mystery" published three months after "A Scandal in Bohemia."

Once again, Holmes and Watson are travelling to their destination in a first-class railway carriage. Holmes is reading his 'pocket Petrarch.' What's intriguing about this is that Petrarch's most famous poems were about his chaste love for a woman beyond his reach. [5]

"the soul leaves the heart to follow you;

and with much thought he then unravels."
"This hope sustained me once:
now she is missing, and I spend too much time in her." [6]

It is my assertion that Irene influenced Sherlock's image of women through her singular beauty, her grace, her spectacular musical talent, and, notably, her keen intelligence. As an opera star, she enjoyed a freedom most women of her day did not. Societal norms significantly constrained and controlled women's lives in Victorian England.

Sherlock Holmes was an enlightened gentleman with the unique understanding his intelligence and world view afforded of the classism and sexism of his day. And how these strictures imperilled the lives of women and men. How the need to conform to this societal inhumanity defiled and twisted people's true natures. Holmes would see, more than any other male, how Irene Adler is free of this, how she determines her own life in every way. Along with everything else she is, this would intrigue him. As the celebrated diva, Irene would have been pursued by men all over Europe, in the cities of opera: Paris, Vienna, Prague, Rome, Florence, London, Dublin, Warsaw, St. Petersburg, and even the Kingdom of Bohemia.

Her farewell letter was addressed to Mr Sherlock Holmes, and not the King. In it she lifted the veil from his "dear, kind old clergyman." Unmasking Holmes after he engineered the faux fire in her Briony Lodge home. Further that she and her husband had a marriage of equals, "We both thought the best resource was flight—I love and am loved by a better man." Even in marriage, Irene was her own woman.

Of Irene Adler, the Adventuresses of Sherlock Holmes purport that, "she has become an icon of feminine independence, style, and resourcefulness…" [7]

Leslie S. Klinger holds that Holmes's feelings towards Adler, "eventually form a startling contrast to the accepted picture of Holmes."

As a woman author of Sherlock Holmes novels, I say, "Thank God!" [8]

Given that Baker Street was just down the road from Serpentine Avenue, Irene disguised herself and popped down to No. 221B for confirmation of her assertion. Yet, as the superb performer used to taking many curtain calls, she could not resist addressing him.

It is my hypothesis that what ensued, and Madam Adler-Norton's letter to Sherlock Holmes, is proof that their playful exchange was more suited to lovers than to adversaries.

My author's unconventional perspective and additions to Doyle's story are presented below. For the sake of clarity, the narrator's point of view has been changed to that of Sherlock Holmes. He has realised the truth of Mike Brosnan's postulation, that "Holmes missed out on a good thing when he let *the* woman get away." [9]

In the end, Sherlock Holmes would be energised by what he perceived as the successful completion of his plans. Could the Great Detective then stand staring on the threshold of No. 221B Baker Street wondering about who penetrated his defences? I think not.

Watson and I had reached Baker Street and had stopped at the door. I was searching my pockets for the keys when someone passing said,

"Good night, Mr Sherlock Holmes."

There were several people on the pavement at the time, but the greeting appeared to come from a slim youth in an ulster who had hurried by.

"I've heard that voice before," I said, staring down the dimly lit street.

My thoughts flashed by in an instant. *Is my fame now at the level of strangers greeting me in the street? Ridiculous, I am still in disguise! There is but one person who might unmask me.*

I left Watson at our door, raced in pursuit, and drew up next to the boy. Revealing Irene in men's dress, I smiled, offered my arm, and said, "Madam Norton."

Flushed with her exercise and her dare, she struck out at me and ran to her carriage, which was waiting near Regent's Park.

A few strides and I joined her there.

"Madam Norton, I will not detain you, as I only want a chance to speak with you."

"Sir, you are a formidable antagonist! Unhand me and let me go!"

"Thank you for your compliment, Irene. Surely you have surmised my rationale for leaving behind the King's photograph?"

I delivered her into her carriage. As I hoped, she gestured for me to leap in as well. Her driver turned the horses into the park while I removed my clergyman's wig and facial hair.

"You arranged for all those milling people on Serpentine Avenue, just to be taken into Bryony Lodge, did you not? And that smoke rocket to trick me?"

"Yes, and disguised myself, used theatrical paint to simulate blood. A wound that you attended with such graceful gentleness." Again, I took her hand.

"I am newly married, sir."

"It was I who witnessed your marriage, Irene. Oh, that I would have stopped it from happening. But when on a case I am intensely single-minded."

"Why didn't you simply ring my doorbell?"

"Madam Norton, you are a prodigious adversary. Yet, it has been a joy to observe your brilliant ingenuity in this affair."

"Flowers or jewellery usually accompanied a proposal.' She displayed her ring. 'But I am already married, Mr Holmes. Godfrey is waiting for me."

"There is still time, Irene. With no other woman, would I wish to spend my life. Your supreme intelligence, your cunning, I could share a lifetime delighting in your heavenly contralto. You could continue your career as I will. I believe the suffragists have created an egalitarian marriage contract, perfect for two of such accomplishments. Don't you think?"

"Buy a flower, sir, buy a flower?" A flower seller's basket appeared at the window of our carriage. I bought the lot and presented it with a flourish to Irene.

"I will put an end to the King's pursuit and you will be free, Madam Norton."

"Laughing, she said, 'Mr Holmes, this is most out of character for such an intrepid sleuth. You might join me on stage with such acting talent. On tour, I have turned down several intriguing proposals. Yet, I find it difficult to believe yours is not another deception.'"

"For such an unconventional woman, Madam, you are behaving in a most commonplace way. Marriage to me would embrace that eccentricity you so clearly prefer."

"It is too late! I have made my choice. As a gentleman, you should know this. Forgive me, but my husband expects me."

She reached across to open the carriage door. I knew I had but a moment to impress her with my true feelings. As so many have shared in a London carriage, I gently encircled her with my arms and kissed her. She did not push me away. In fact, to my happy surprise, she returned the kiss.

I leapt out as she signalled to her driver to exit the park. And wistfully watched Madam Norton's carriage disappear into traffic as it continued up the hill to St. John's Wood.

Crossing from the park into Baker Street, I put my key in the lock and climbed to the first-floor sitting room. The house was peaceful. Watson was sleeping in Baker Street that night. Mrs Hudson had gone to bed hours ago. I took up my violin and dreamily played the song I heard in my mind, the chorale Irene sang while I was on watch at Briony Lodge. Afterwards,

I readied myself for the drama yet to be played on the morning's stage. My costume would be an impeccable London gentleman's knee-length black frock-coat and topper. This time, I would call upon Irene in my own person.

Early next morning, Watson and I were engaged upon our toast and coffee when the King of Bohemia rushed into the room.

"You have really got it!" he cried, grasping me by either shoulder and looking eagerly into my face.

"Not yet."

"But you have hopes?"

"I have hopes."

"Then, come. I am all impatience to be gone."

"We must have a cab."

"No, my brougham is waiting."

"Then that will simplify matters."

"We descended and started off once more for Briony Lodge."

"Irene Adler is married," I remarked.

"Married! When?"

"Yesterday."

"But to whom?"

"To an English lawyer named Norton."

"But she could not love him?"

"I am in hopes that she does."

"And why in hopes?"

"Because it would spare Your Majesty all fear of future annoyance. If the lady loves her husband, she does not love Your Majesty. If she does not love Your Majesty, there is no reason why she should interfere with Your Majesty's plan."

"It is true. And yet! Well! I wish she had been of my own station! What a queen she would have made!"

He relapsed into a moody silence which was not broken until we drew up in Serpentine Avenue.

The door of Briony Lodge was open, and an elderly woman stood upon the steps. She watched us with a sardonic eye as we stepped from the brougham.

"Mr Sherlock Holmes, I believe?" said she.

"I am Mr Holmes," I answered, looking at her with a questioning and rather startled gaze.

"Indeed! My mistress told me that you were likely to call. She left this morning with her husband, by the 5:15 train from Charing Cross, for the Continent."

"What!' I staggered back, with chagrin and surprise. 'Do you mean that she has left England?"

"Never to return."

"And the papers?' asked the King hoarsely. 'All is lost."

"We shall see."

I pushed past the servant, and rushed into the drawing-room, followed by the King and Watson. The furniture was scattered about in every direction, with dismantled shelves, and open drawers, as if the lady had hurriedly ransacked them before her flight. I rushed at the bell-pull, tore back a small sliding shutter, and, plunging in my hand, pulled out a photograph and a letter. The photograph was of Irene Adler herself in evening dress, the letter was superscribed to "Sherlock Holmes, Esq. To be left till called for."

I tore it open and we all three read it together. It was dated at midnight of the preceding night, and ran in this way:

"MY DEAR MR SHERLOCK HOLMES,

You really did it very well. You took me in completely. Until after the alarm of fire, I had not a suspicion. But then, when I found how I had betrayed myself, I began to think. I had been warned against you months ago. I had been told that if the King employed an agent, it would certainly be you. And your address had been given me. Yet, with all this, you made me reveal what you wanted to know. Even after I became suspicious, I found it hard to think evil of such a dear, kind old clergyman. But, you know, I have been trained as an actress myself. Male costume is nothing new to me. I often take advantage of the freedom which it gives. I sent John, the coachman, to watch you, ran upstairs, got into my walking clothes, as I call them, and came down just as you departed.

"Well, I followed you to your door, and so made sure that I was really an object of interest to the celebrated Mr Sherlock Holmes. Then I, rather imprudently, wished you good night, and started for the Temple to see my husband.

"We both thought the best resource was flight when pursued by so formidable an antagonist; so you will find the nest empty when you call tomorrow. As to the photograph, your client may rest in peace. I love and am loved by a better man than he. The King may do what he will without hindrance from one whom he has cruelly wronged. I keep it only to safeguard myself, and to preserve a weapon which will always secure me from any steps which he might take in the future. I leave a photograph which he might care to possess; and I remain, dear Mr Sherlock Holmes,

Very truly yours,

IRENE NORTON, née ADLER"

"What a woman - oh, what a woman!' cried the King of Bohemia, when we had all three read this epistle. 'Did I not tell you how quick and resolute she was? Would she not have made an admirable queen? Is it not a pity she was not on my level?"

"From what I have seen of the lady, she seems, indeed, to be on a very different level to Your Majesty,' I said coldly. 'I am sorry that I have not been able to bring Your Majesty's business to a more successful conclusion."

"On the contrary, my dear sir,' cried the King. 'Nothing could be more successful. I know that her word is inviolate. The photograph is now as safe as if it were in the fire."

"I am glad to hear Your Majesty say so."

"I am immensely indebted to you. Pray tell me in what way I can reward you. This ring–" He slipped an emerald snake ring from his finger and held it out upon the palm of his hand.

"Your Majesty has something which I should value even more highly," I said.

"You have but to name it."

"This photograph!'"

"The King stared at me in amazement."

"Irene's photograph!' he cried. 'Certainly, if you wish it."

"I thank Your Majesty. Then there is no more to be done in the matter. I have the honour to wish you a very good morning." I bowed and, turning away from the King's outstretched hand, Watson and I set off for my chambers.

The narrative Watson was presently penning left much to be desired. Conflicting statements about myself and my humanity filled its opening. Described in this fashion, one would want to influence the writer away from such embellishment. Yet getting a message to Irene was the more important. It necessitated clarity and precision to turn the tables.

I foresaw that a story about the marriage of such an illustrious opera diva could flood the world's magazines and newspapers. No matter where she and her husband settled, my disguised missive would find her.

The distinct variation between the first paragraph and the last carried an alternative message to one as brilliant as Irene. She would discover that she was the catalyst which provoked a substantial change in my life. That I kept her photograph as a token could only be seen as a plain statement of my affection.

During that morning's walk down to Baker Street, I addressed him,

"Watson, no doubt you will chronicle this little adventure for public consumption. I would ask you to inform your readers how my best plans were beaten by a woman's wit.

That I used to make merry over the cleverness of women, but you have not heard me do it of late. And when I speak of Irene Adler, or when I refer to her photograph, it is always under the honourable title of *the* woman. Do you understand, Watson?"

Whaling-EXPRESS.CO.UK [1]

Black Peter's Misplaced Mariners

"There in the middle of it was the man himself, his face twisted like a lost soul in hell, and his great brindled beard stuck upwards in his agony. Right through his broad breast a steel harpoon had been driven, and it had sunk deep into the wood of the wall behind him." The Adventure of Black Peter. [2]

Of the many fruitful cases Sherlock Holmes and I have brought to conclusion since his return from the Reichenbach Fall, this for me was one of the most compelling. Certainly, murder by whale harpoon was not an everyday occurrence in Sussex.

Early in July 1895, Holmes and I were called away by Inspector Stanley Hopkins to solve an adventure as bloody as any in our association and as singular as each of them when Black Peter came to our attention.

This case brought us face to face with the brutal and courageous whale-hunting fraternity. As this was a favourite subject of mine, "The Adventure of Black Peter" was one I truly enjoyed writing up.

But this is not that story. As the chronicler of Sherlock Holmes's cases, my mail of late has been rife with accusations as to the state of my memory. This, I dearly hope, is a clearing up of certain questions left unanswered.

On this last morning, after ten days of involvement, we awaited the arrival of Inspector Hopkins to our Baker Street rooms. Holmes, Hopkins and I would shortly bring the matter to completion. Sherlock Holmes was occupied with setting the stage for its true climax. As the tantalising smells of Mrs. Hudson's breakfast preparations wafted up to our sitting room, I was organising my notes. For though the case would finish today, my penning of the adventure was just beginning.

There were three mysteries to this story: Who killed Black Peter? What happened to Nelligan? And what of the two sailors in Holmes's room? Sherlock Holmes solved the first two by the singular application of his magnificent methods. And in the heat of the moment, I undertook to clarify the last.

Arctic Whale Captains were knowledgeable men: explorers, scientists, authors, and clergymen. Captain Peter Carey, or Black Peter as he was known to all who served with him, was none of these. He was a sailor to the blood, fearless on the sea and the deck of his ship. The S.S. Sea Unicorn always made port. From Dundee on the Scottish coast, his only justice was death over the Unicorn's side.

He hunted the Bowhead Whale off the coast of Greenland. The accommodating Bowhead swims slowly, floats after death, and has the largest baleen of any whale. Versatile baleen was used in carriage springs, corset stays, fishing rods, hoops for women's dresses, frames for travelling bags, trunks, women's hats, and buggy whips. The ship arrived mid-summer when the ice had melted enough for passage and sailed out in late summer to avoid being trapped in the ice. This cruel occupation brought to our civilised world the precious oil locked in the bodies of seals and whales. The oil perilously recovered lit our streets, our humble homes, and grand palaces. A necessity of our civilised world.

These valiant seamen faced the mighty whale in boats tiny against the animal's bulk. They rode astride the bow, their legs braced against the thighboard, with only forged iron-headed harpoons in their powerful arms and the shark-filled watery depths below. Each harpooner could aim and sink a hardwood stave of 'whale iron' into their prey by matching the roll and crash of their craft to the death throes of a leviathan.

"Watson, did you know whales have acute hearing?" Holmes asked, turning towards me as he pulled a written paper from his desk drawer.

I looked up from my writing, disbelieving my ears.

"How did you —? Never mind."

"My friend, how many times must I relate to you your expressive face and my deductive abilities?' he said as he palmed a matchbox. 'It adds more jeopardy to the whalers' job. They must row noiselessly as well as expeditiously as possible to their terrifying game. Or else it will dive and be gone.'"

"You amaze me, Holmes."

"This is a story I would enjoy reading, my friend."

He lit a cigarette and returned to his duties.

These men were also sealers. And this was a grim and bloody job. Captain Carey anchored his Sea Unicorn at the unstable Arctic ice pans. The hunters disembarked with their long gaffs to catch and slaughter walruses, harp seals, and hooded seals. Leaving themselves exhausted and the snow scarlet with blood. This hunt carried its own difficulties, long hours, shifting ice, erratic storms, and the hauling of hundreds of seals back to the Unicorn. Ship's cook spent his days clanging metal pots to broadcast their location to sailors lost in fog and dangerous weather, or stranded on the ice foes.

My involvement in this story began with Holmes's dramatic arrival at our hallway door. I will never forget his startling entrance as he ducked to clear the lintel and poised for my inspection. Not only had he not hung his hat, but under his arm was a six-foot-long barbed harpoon.

That very day, we surveyed the horrible crime scene with Inspector Hopkins. Holmes, under the dockyard alias of Captain Basil, put alternative events in motion that would surely lure the killer to our very rooms.

Now, Holmes rose to clean his long-stemmed pipe and travelled to my tobacco pouch to fill it. He laughed and slapped me on the back.

"Ha! Watson, you were so flummoxed when I appeared for breakfast that morning! I wish I had a camera." He laughed again.

"Holmes, this is insufferable!" I said.

"I failed at the butcher's that morning, humorously attempting to thrust a piece of metal and wood through that dead pig. You wouldn't call me a weak man, would you, Watson?"

"Holmes, you are one of the strongest men I know."

"Thank you, Doctor. For me, it was an impossible feat. Yet, for the Sea Unicorn's harpooner, his many voyages would build his arm the way nothing else could."

When all was said and done, we discovered Black Peter had met his nemesis in an old shipmate intent on blackmail. Scotland Yard was bamboozled as to the true solution of the case, and Hopkins had arrested the wrong man.

This morning, Inspector Hopkins joined us at Baker Street. Holmes was dressed as a sailor down to the boots. His jacket and hat with Captain's insignia were slung over the back of a chair.

"As to this terrible person of yours, where is he, Holmes?" said Hopkins.

"I rather fancy that he is on the stair," said Sherlock Holmes. "I think, Watson, that you would do well to put that revolver where you can reach it."

He rose, dressed in his jacket, and laid the paper upon a side-table.

"Now we are ready," said he.

Mrs Hudson opened the door to say that there were three men inquiring for Captain Basil.

"Thank you, Mrs Hudson. Show them in one by one," he said.

Holmes informed the first two men that the berth was full, gave them each a half-sovereign, and asked them to wait in the next room. Those familiar with my stories and my determination to portray accurate descriptions knew that besides our sitting room, the only other room on the first-floor in Baker Street was Holmes's bedroom. So, naturally, much of the following narrative took place there.

James Lancaster entered our sitting room. He was a small ruddy man with white side-whiskers, and superstitious in the way of sailors. Sent to wait in the next room, he opened the door to Holmes's bedroom and looked in. The morning window light had filtered through our shade tree. Lancaster sat on the sole chair. Then, looking around at the faces of criminals decorating the walls, he pulled out his rabbit's foot as Captain Basil closed the door.

Hugh Pattins was the second seaman, tall, thin, and unhealthy-looking. From the bedroom, Lancaster could hear him as he answered the Captain's questions, and he too was ushered into the bedroom. As the door closed, Pattins threw himself onto Holmes's bed and lay with his hands behind his head. He found cigarettes and a match on the side table and lit one.

Then he spoke to Lancaster, "This isn't a bad thing. Is there anything to drink in here?"

"No, I don't think so."

"Relax, it's a comfortable place, Lancaster. Have a cigarette?"

"Don't you see? All those beasty eyes! They follow you around. Don't you see them?" He pointed to Holmes's framed criminal studies.

Pattins lit a candle and proceeded to the frames, shining its light upon them as he circled the walls of the room.

"Just queer pictures. What would Cap'n Basil want with the likes of them? Old crewmates? They don't look much like sailors. Oh, here's one! Look, Lancaster, do ye know him?"

The little sailor moved to the picture, shook his head, and ran back to his chair.

"Once, I served on a ship out of Nantucket. Our Indian harpooner from America refused to be in any photographs. He said they stole your soul. Maybe that's what these pictures are – not photographs but souls. Maybe he's the devil he is?"

"You don't have to look."

"Can't help it," Lancaster said, "they might move."

Pattins laughed. "What a pigeon-livered ratbag I have for a mate! I suppose ye won't be going down to the pub tonight."

"I'll be there. I'm not sitting shut up here with this half-sovereign in my pocket."

"There must be a reason we're locked in here," said Pattins.

"You're crazy! We're not locked in. I'll walk out this door anytime I want. You are a strange one thinkin' we're locked in. Nobody said that—just invited us to wait."

"Then why don't you walk out?"

"Why don't you?"

"He told us to wait."

"Maybe Cap'n Basil's changed his mind?"

"What's the first thing you recall about him?" said Lancaster.

"What are you on about? When?"

"Today, now."

"The first thing?"

"Yes."

"His generosity." Pattins took the Captain's half-sovereign from his pocket.

"Heads or tails?"

Pattins flipped it into the air, caught it, and slapped it onto the back of his hand.

"Heads!"

"Ack—like the heads all around us! He's the dickens, I tell you!" said Lancaster.

"Naw, ole Black Peter was the man to be feared. He truly was the devil. Kill ye as soon as look at ye. I'd give this half-sovereign to shake the hand of the man who harpooned him to a wall."

He flipped the coin again and slapped his palm over it.

"Ye want to bet its tails?"

"Just by flippin' a coin, you aim to win my newly acquired wealth? Nothing doing."

Pattins slipped it into his pocket and walked to the window.

"Just passin' the time. Look here, Cap'n Basil's cabin is due north." He pointed out the window.

"They say good navigators are sensitive to polestars, like whales. I can feel it. Always facing north is a good position for an Arctic Sea Cap'n."

"Did he ask you your rank?"

"I never got a chance to tell him. It's for my eyes too. They hire me. Cap'n trusts my eyes. It's easy to get lost when a harpooned whale is towing a little whaleboat at 20 miles-per-hour out to sea. Here is where my skills are prized. I always find my way back to the ship." He stood straighter.

"I'm proof I haven't lost one yet!"

"He didn't ask mine, either."

Pattins slapped Lancaster on the back.

"Cooks are shopkeepers left behind on the ship. Anyway, it's on your papers. Me, I join the rowers launching the whaleboats. Aye, you miss all the adventure!"

"And a good deal of the danger, too." Lancaster said, "Cutting blubber into 'Bible leaves' and boiling it down to oil while beating the sharks to what's left has its own peril. But if we aren't hired on as crew, why are we still here?"

Pattins added a pillow and relaxed into Holmes's bed. Found another cigarette and lit it, blowing the smoke at his roommate.

"Maybe he thinks if the harpooner is acceptable, he will bring in others. And that's us."

"Didn't you shake his hand, Pattins? There was power in it. And those cold grey eyes lookin' through me." He shuddered. "I'd swear he could see down to my very soul."

"Naw, you're off your chump! It was a good handshake. Cap'n Basil must be one of them who's always on the lookout to discover a new type of animal, or plant, or man and put his name on it. Aye, that's what he was. That's more like it."

He picked up a newspaper from the carpet. Lancaster, with a candle in his hand, looked under the bed.

"No rope."

Then around the hearth.

"A good stout poker."

He climbed on the chair and searched the top of the armoire.

"Nothing."

Then opened the doors, blew out the candle, and climbed inside.

"Can't you sit and rest? Is there a flask in one of those jackets?"

Pattin's turned the leaves of the paper. From within the depths of the large armoire, the little sailor spoke.

"It's cedar, smell it! Don't they make eternity boxes out of it?" Pattins said, "Whalers and sealers never make it to a box. We're shark food over the side of a ship."

"Sometimes, when the ship is locked-in fog or ice, all I can think of is, 'Is this it?'"

Lancaster stepped out and then explored the drawers.

"With the flag at half-mast, is only right."

He closed the armoire doors and looked out the window.

"On a clear blue day. The whole crew on deck. The Cap'n and Mate saluting in uniform."

"Would you be happy with that?"

"Yes, the flag at half-mast, yes, that would make me happy."

"It's the luck of our profession."

"The blessings."

"The prospects. £100."

Lancaster said, "But Cap'n Basil told us there are no berths. Why'd he put us in here? Why not just let us go? That's what I keep asking myself."

Pattins smoked. "We are here with money in our pockets and tobacco to smoke. And in time, we will be on our way down to the public."

"It's inevitable. But it wouldn't hurt to prepare."

"For the inevitable?"

Pattins laughed and threw his cigarette into the fireplace. Poured water into the basin and washed his face and hands.

"Maybe it's just his bloody way?"

"To kennel us like dogs?"

"Lucky dogs!"

"But he already dismissed us, paid us for our time. Why keep us?"

Lancaster continued his search and opened the other side of the armoire.

"Pattins, look at this. Now you see proof there's a devil on the other side of that door!"

He stabbed his finger in the direction of the sitting room.

"Scalps, hair and beards!"

He threw one at Pattins, who gingerly caught it.

"Don't you have anything in that head?" He turned it inside out. "It's a wig. Look here, there's stitching and glue."

He held it to Lancaster, who batted it away.

"Noses! What the blazes kind of man collects noses? I ask you. Is he a dandy, do city women like this? A seaman's clothes, a striped jacket and a straw boater, a Chinese blouse, a preacher's black suit, and widow's weeds. Hey, look at me!"

Lancaster, wearing a straw hat, sings in a fine tenor voice while continued to assess the inside of the armoire.

"The winds blew up, her bow dipped down. Oh blow, my bully boys, blow—What's this?"

Lancaster uncovered the grotesquery.

"Hogmagundy! It's the monstrous skull of one of his victims! A bullet right through it. This is a warning, that's what it is. We need to leave now!"

"Looks a little like him. Stop your caterwauling! Cap'n's are a strange lot; they have their own fancies. Like you, Lancaster. Leave them clothes alone. Unless you plan on tying them together, it betokens nothing. Go find us a good hempen rope so we can back-slang it."

Lancaster hung the hat on the skull and closed the armoire doors.

Pattins put his boots up on the footboard.

"You know the Cap'n prob'ly needs time to discuss it with his first mate. Since we came one on top of the other, there was no time for it."

"So we wait."

Lancaster went to the window and looked out.

"It doesn't look far. For two sailors, I mean, just a leap into the garden. If we only had something to tie. You see, there's a way out the back."

Pattins joined him and leaned out the window.

It was then that the third and last man, Patrick Cairns, entered the sitting room. Lancaster and Pattins had waited with him on the stairs. The enormous harpooner saluted the Captain and stood sailor-fashion, as had both men before him.

Through the door, the masterful voice of Captain Basil was heard to question the harpooner. He explained the duties aboard his ship. Then all was quiet in the sitting room. Pattins lay back in the bed and foraged for a box of matches.

"Did you find any matches in that cabinet?"

"No. Pattins, I think we should leave."

Lancaster looked out the window and continued his scrutiny for something they could tie and make fast. He pulled at the bed covering. Pattins swatted Lancaster's hand.

"Be off!" He lit another cigarette.

In the next room, the voices began again. The unmistakable bellow of the ungainly giant could be heard through the door.

"Shall I sign here?"

"This will do." Captain Basil said.

Then a click of steel and a sound like an enraged bull. In the next instant, Captain Basil and the enormous sailor were rolling on the floor. Substantial furniture was smashed, and their contents pitched and crashed to the floor. Holmes would be adding a good deal to our rent this month.

It must be said that even with Inspector Hopkins on hand, this harpooner was a man far beyond all of us in size and strength. A man used to wrestling with a 50-ton whale was not a man to be taken lightly. Yet, Holmes expended no thought upon this aspect. He put everything in motion and trusted to the men he called in. This time it was Hopkins, and myself who supported his leap into the fray at the moment of valour.

As Holmes fastened the darbies to the harpooner's wrists, he had his arms on either side of Cairn's neck. The next we knew; the sailor raised his arms together and released from the grasp of his captor. Holmes tripped the giant and leapt onto him. The seaman attempted to pummel Holmes with his handcuffed fists to achieve his escape. Holmes flipped out of the way of those terrible arms and fixed a scissor hold around the sailor's neck with his powerful legs. Hopkins then threw himself across the man's body to keep his hands immobilised.

Holmes's cry, "WATSON!" caused the cocking of my pistol at Cairn's temple. The cold steel of my revolver successfully stopped the harpooner. Finally, Holmes and Hopkins lashed his ankles with cord.

During the fracas, Pattins opened the bedroom door a crack, looked in at the hullabaloo, and then closed it quickly, addressing the cook.

"Stop your worrying, Lancaster, nobody saw me. They were too preoccupied with their wrestling. Cap'n Basil's battling the harpooner tooth and nail—and he is winning. He already has the darbies on his wrists. And the other one has a gun."

Lancaster jumped to his feet and ran to the window. He whispered, "I worry if it is to be our fate also."

"What did we do? Nothing!"

"Shh, be more quiet! But don't you see we've got to escape before they come for us?"

He wrung his hands and looked around at the pictures.

"If the harpooner is treated that way, what do you think they'll do to us? One's a bleeding Bobbie, the other's the devil and his accomplice. Who knows what their sinister plans may be? We're caught in a web, like characters in a play!"

Pattins shook his head and stepped to the door. The two sailors listened intently for the words of Captain Basil.

"I must really apologise, Inspector Hopkins," said Holmes.

"I fear that the scrambled eggs are cold. However, you will enjoy the rest of your breakfast all the better, will you not, for the thought that you have brought your case to a triumphant conclusion?"

The two seamen never heard Stanley Hopkins answer, nor the Black Maria Van that came for Patrick Cairns. Once everything was tied tight, Hugh Pattins pushed past James Lancaster and escaped first. Lancaster watched his descent, collected himself, considered once again escaping out the hall door, then with many complaints under his breath, he heaved himself out the window. Lancaster swung, holding to the end of the blanket and slid down to the bottom, leaving some skin off the palm of his hand, then jumped the last six feet to the ground. They followed along the backs of houses for a way out. North of the Public House, they found an alleyway into the street.

Pattins said, "When was the last time you shipped out, Lancaster? Those weak legs of yours haven't climbed rigging in many months, and your hands are soft as blubber!"

He stood to his full height. "Cooks cook!"

"I don't relish any of your belly timber." He laughed.

Lancaster laughed with him, "It's not the Savoy, but I do my best." He pointed. "There's the way out. Come on. I won't feel safe 'til we reach the docks."

At our sitting-room table, Sherlock Holmes contemplated his cold breakfast, then laughed heartily.

"Watson, I would have enjoyed taking the battle to its conclusion. The finesse of technique over brute strength."

"Holmes, I know you are a prodigious boxer. But all it would take is one landed punch from a man used to battling whales to lay you out."

"At any rate, he would have much to teach me."

"This morning's capture of the murderous harpooner was marvellous, Holmes!"

He looked up suddenly like a hound listening for the view-halloo.

"Excuse me, but in the enthusiasm of subduing Mr Cairns' pugilistic endeavours, it seems we have completely neglected our other guests."

He brushed off his trousers, smoothed his hair and straightened his tie.

"What a careless host I have been!"

Holmes jovially addressed them, "Please forgive me, gentlemen. Will you join us in some breakfast in compensation for your long wait?"

There was no answer.

Sherlock Holmes opened wide the door to his bedroom.

What we found was an open window in an empty room. A bedsheet and blanket were rigged to each other, attached to the armoire and billowing like a sail out the window. He leaned out, pulled them in, detached the end from the armoire, and rolled them into a bundle.

We lifted his furniture back against the wall. He turned to me.

"Thank you, Doctor—A sailor's escape? These bowline knots in my bedding certainly proclaims it. Ha! Possibly they assumed what they overheard was forthcoming for them?" He shook his head.

Holmes opened his side door and called out into the hall, "Mrs. Hudson!"

He picked up the wig from the floor and noted the cigarettes, ashes, and his rifled armoire.

"They were curious, but not thieves."

He set things to right. When Mrs. Hudson arrived, she accepted his dirty sheet and blanket.

"Mrs. Hudson, it seems our guests had a more pressing commitment. You will find that one of the gentlemen who descended out my window with the help of my linens slipped down with such velocity that he wore the skin off his hand. At your convenience, please bring up a pot of hot coffee? Thank you."

I looked out the window, then closed it.

"The probability is that they are far away by now, Watson."

Holmes replaced the cigarettes and matches on his bedside table. He moved to our Baker Street windows, pulled out a map and spread it out to catch the light.

He waved me over.

"Watson, I recently sent down to Stanford's for this map of Norway. Come, let us plan our trip."

"Holmes, they left by your bedroom window? Sailors are used to climbing. They must either come out by the Post Office or the pub. I shall see if I might catch them," I said and ran out the door and down to the street.

Engrossed in the map, Holmes grunted at me, "A fine deduction, Watson."

In my role as chronicler, filling out the particulars of this story required some unusual extra-curricular research. However, once I found the right dockside pub, the rest was simple.

With my revolver pocketed, I rushed after the sailors. The seamen emerged from the back of the Public House into Park Lane. First, the tall one, followed by the shorter one running to catch up. Both headed south at a fast pace. Possibly towards the St. Katherine's Docks. I followed in a hansom. The little man had worryingly caught sight of me and elbowed his taller partner, who waved him away.

Indeed, when we arrived at the River Thames, it was the Truelove Public House on Church Lane. They entered as if coming home.

I left my cab and shadowed them into the pub, my tweeds and cap easily blending in. Though mine were considerably cleaner. The two sailors split up, each to his own. I took a seat near James Lancaster and ordered a pint.

After quickly emptying his tankard, Mr Lancaster clapped it on the table so the audience could appreciate its emptiness. He began his story just loud enough to herald the initiation of his performance. It seemed this was expected, as the noise hushed around him. He upturned his cap and again clapped his empty crockery. As it turned out, the smaller sailor had the larger voice.

"Black Peter's gone!"

The pub's complement hooted and cheered.

"You've heard of his grisly death? Got his due, he did! Half pirate he was. How many of you felt his knife at your throat?"

He looked around. "Aye's" filled the room.

"As have I. But don't think you can rest. Don't drop your guard, he's not the last of the line! Cruel bloodthirsty Cap'ns never seem to go down. Always another to take their place."

He slapped the table.

"It's a warning I'm weaving with this tale. Beware! The terrible story of the colossal, cadaverous sea Cap'n, a giant, wreathed in pipe smoke of the foulest kind. He lured the best seamen to their doom. His mind was as sharp as a sealer's knife, but his heart was darker than ole Black Peter's!"

The pub dwellers groaned.

"This was a cany Cap'n. His steel-grey eyes reached into your soul and tore out your secrets. I think him the devil, but you can tell me what you think when my story's done.

He pointed out to his audience.

"Not one of you has enough will to withstand that fiend's torturous gaze."

He slowly looked around at them.

"I saw him. Was tested by him. I watched him best the most powerful harpooner. All of this is true!" He coughed.

"But I'm afraid I won't be able to finish my story," He coughed again. "My whistle's dry."

I directed the landlord to place another pint in front of him.

"Thank you, sir," he drank deeply and began again.

"This Cap'n always returned with more barrels of oil than any other. And why? Because the oil was as good as gold to him. If you slip on the blubbery deck, it's to the sharks you'll go. Woe to any man lost on the ice; it was only death that found him.

"He searched the seas for strange men and animals, and these he would dry or shrink for display. Have you never laid eyes on those shrunken, wizened faces? Just one look can stop your heart dead in your chest.

"Believe me. This Sea Cap'n's voice was as deep as the sea, his growls louder than the roars of a thousand trumpeting walruses. He could read your thoughts and could hypnotise the strongest and most leery man. I saw it with my own eyes!

199

No one could outfox this Cap'n. A mesmerist, he was. Woe to those who came under his power. There was no escape!

"He knew every language, so couldn't be fooled. He had a sharp dog's smeller, could see in the dark like a cat, and moved like a leopard silently going in for the kill. His hearing and sight were like the great swooping raptors. Believe me or not! It was all true.

"No locks could contain him. He was a deadeye shot with a pistol. One bullet was all he needed. Never beaten, he mastered every form of hand fighting ever invented. He had the power to transform into a monstrous beast. With teeth like the tiger shark, he wielded a mighty stick with the force of a whale's tail."

Lancaster raised his voice. "With one hand, he could throw a goliath overboard! Beware! If you dared a turn on this ship, you wouldn't never come back!"

He finished his pint, and I bought him another.

"He'd lock away your very being in darkness until your waiting for release caused you to disappear into the very dust of existence," he said, wiping his mouth with his sleeve. "I escaped, but was afraid to disturb it, wondering who might be there."

He smiled and looked out at his audience. They laughed.

"Listen to me, this is no idle warning! On this very day, I watched as he bested Patrick Cairns, the harpooner! Tied him up and served him to the bloody mutton shunters, he did."

His audience groaned and shouted curses.

"I was next, but I escaped with my life! You may not be so lucky.

"This fearsome Cap'n hung horrible photos on the walls of his cabin, the souls of lost, tortured, or dead shipmates. The gruesome photos were taken at the height of their torture, their very death throes. The deeply sunken eyes, bruised noses, browned teeth, and blackened mouths howled in silent agony. Their eyes seemed to follow you and their sneers whispered, 'Beware, BEWARE, the wrath of Cap'n Basil!"

His listeners cheered, laughed, whistled, dropped coins in his cap, and moved on. After more refreshment and a fiver, it was here that Lancaster gave me a full reckoning of his and Pattins's doings in Holmes's bedroom that morning.

I replaced my pocketbook in my jacket and watched as a tall, thin, elderly man in sailor's garb separated himself from the crowd. He was coming our way, with a pair of keen eyes overhung by bushy white brows, long grey whiskers, and a horrible cough. His back was bowed, and his legs were bandied. I diagnosed his painful breathing as he dropped a coin in Lancaster's cap, sat at my table, lit his short clay pipe, and tipped his hat to me.

I ordered pints. He nodded his thanks, took a long drink, and spoke.

"Watson, I'm afraid you have competition, old man." And he cackled.

"Holmes! How did you get here?"

"You know, I never realised the great dividends available from your calling, my friend. For the rest of our days, we will never be dry in a pub again!"

Frederic Dorr Steele. "The Adventure Of Black Peter."

"The Adventure Of Black Peter"

Sir Arthur Conan Doyle

First published March 1904 in *The Strand Magazine*.
Presented here unabridged for your enjoyment.

I have never known my friend to be in better form, both mental and physical, than in the year '95. His increasing fame had brought with it an immense practice, and I should be guilty of an indiscretion if I were even to hint at the identity of some of the illustrious clients who crossed our humble threshold in Baker Street. Holmes, however, like all great artists, lived for his art's sake, and save in the case of the Duke of Holdernesse, I have seldom known him claim any large reward for his inestimable services. So unworldly was he—or so capricious—that he frequently refused his help to the powerful and wealthy where the problem made no appeal to his sympathies, while he would devote weeks of most intense application to the affairs of some humble client whose case presented those strange and dramatic qualities which appealed to his imagination and challenged his ingenuity.

In this memorable year '95 a curious and incongruous succession of cases had engaged his attention, ranging from his famous investigation of the sudden death of Cardinal Tosca—an inquiry which was carried out by him at the express desire of His Holiness the Pope—down to his arrest of Wilson, the notorious canary-trainer, which removed a plague-spot from the East-End of London. Close on the heels of these two famous cases came the tragedy of Woodman's Lee, and the very obscure circumstances which surrounded the death of Captain Peter Carey. No record of the doings of

Mr Sherlock Holmes would be complete which did not include some account of this very unusual affair.

During the first week of July my friend had been absent so often and so long from our lodgings that I knew he had something on hand. The fact that several rough-looking men called during that time and inquired for Captain Basil made me understand that Holmes was working somewhere under one of the numerous disguises and names with which he concealed his own formidable identity. He had at least five small refuges in different parts of London in which he was able to change his personality. He said nothing of his business to me, and it was not my habit to force a confidence. The first positive sign which he gave me of the direction which his investigation was taking was an extraordinary one. He had gone out before breakfast, and I had sat down to mine, when he strode into the room, his hat upon his head and a huge barbed-headed spear tucked like an umbrella under his arm.

"Good gracious, Holmes!" I cried. "You don't mean to say that you have been walking about London with that thing?"

"I drove to the butcher's and back."

"The butcher's?"

"And I return with an excellent appetite. There can be no question, my dear Watson, of the value of exercise before breakfast. But I am prepared to bet that you will not guess the form that my exercise has taken."

"I will not attempt it."

He chuckled as he poured out the coffee.

"If you could have looked into Allardyce's back shop you would have seen a dead pig swung from a hook in the ceiling, and a gentleman in his shirt-sleeves furiously stabbing at it with this weapon. I was that energetic person, and I have satisfied myself that by no exertion of my strength can I transfix the pig with a single blow. Perhaps you would care to try?"

"Not for worlds. But why were you doing this?"

"Because it seemed to me to have an indirect bearing upon the mystery of Woodman's Lee. Ah, Hopkins, I got your wire last night, and I have been expecting you. Come and join us."

Our visitor was an exceedingly alert man, thirty years of age, dressed in a quiet tweed suit, but retaining the erect bearing of one who was accustomed to official uniform. I recognised him at once as Stanley Hopkins, a young police inspector for whose future Holmes had high hopes, while he in turn professed the admiration and respect of a pupil for the scientific methods of the famous amateur. Hopkins's brow was clouded, and he sat down with an air of deep dejection.

"No, thank you, sir. I breakfasted before I came round. I spent the night in town, for I came up yesterday to report."

"And what had you to report?"

"Failure, sir; absolute failure."

"You have made no progress?"

"None."

"Dear me! I must have a look at the matter."

"I wish to heavens that you would, Mr Holmes. It's my first big chance, and I am at my wit's end. For goodness' sake come down and lend me a hand."

"Well, well, it just happens that I have already read all the available evidence, including the report of the inquest, with some care. By the way, what do you make of that tobacco-pouch found on the scene of the crime? Is there no clue there?"

Hopkins looked surprised.

"It was the man's own pouch, sir. His initials were inside it. And it was of seal-skin—and he an old sealer."

"But he had no pipe."

"No, sir, we could find no pipe; indeed, he smoked very little. And yet he might have kept some tobacco for his friends."

"No doubt. I only mention it because if I had been handling the case I should have been inclined to make that the starting-point of my investigation. However, my friend Dr Watson knows nothing of this matter, and I should be none the worse for hearing the sequence of events once more. Just give us some short sketch of the essentials."

Stanley Hopkins drew a slip of paper from his pocket.

"I have a few dates here which will give you the career of the dead man, Captain Peter Carey. He was born in '45—fifty years of age. He was a most daring and successful seal and whale fisher. In 1883 he commanded the steam sealer SEA UNICORN, of Dundee. He had then had several successful voyages in succession, and in the following year, 1884, he retired. After that he travelled for some years, and finally he bought a small place called Woodman's Lee, near Forest Row, in Sussex. There he has lived for six years, and there he died just a week ago to-day.

"There were some most singular points about the man. In ordinary life he was a strict Puritan—a silent, gloomy fellow. His household consisted of his wife, his daughter, aged twenty, and two female servants. These last were continually changing, for it was never a very cheery situation, and sometimes it became past all bearing. The man was an intermittent drunkard, and when he had the fit on him he was a perfect fiend. He has been known to drive his wife and his daughter out of doors in the middle of the night, and flog them through the park until the whole village outside the gates was aroused by their screams.

"He was summoned once for a savage assault upon the old vicar, who had called upon him to remonstrate with him upon his conduct. In short, Mr Holmes, you would go far before you found a more dangerous man than Peter Carey, and I have heard that he bore the same character when he commanded his ship. He was known in the trade as Black Peter, and the name was given him, not only on account of his swarthy features and the colour of his huge beard, but for the humours which were the terror of all around him. I need not say that he was loathed and avoided by every one of his neighbours, and that I have not heard one single word of sorrow about his terrible end.

"You must have read in the account of the inquest about the man's cabin, Mr Holmes; but perhaps your friend here has not heard of it. He had built himself a wooden outhouse—he always called it 'the cabin'—a few hundred yards from his house, and it was here that he slept every night. It was a little, single-roomed hut, sixteen feet by ten. He kept the key in his pocket, made his own bed, cleaned it himself, and allowed no other foot to cross the threshold. There are small windows on each side, which were covered by curtains and never opened. One of these windows was turned towards the high road, and when the light burned in it at night the folk used to point it out to each other and wonder what Black Peter was doing in there. That's the window, Mr Holmes, which gave us one of the few bits of positive evidence that came out at the inquest.

"You remember that a stonemason, named Slater, walking from Forest Row about one o'clock in the morning— two days before the murder—stopped as he passed the grounds and looked at the square of light still shining among the trees. He swears that the shadow of a man's head turned sideways was clearly visible on the blind, and that this shadow was certainly not that of Peter Carey, whom he knew well. It was that of a bearded man, but the beard was short and bristled forwards in a way very different from that of the captain. So he says, but he had been two hours in the public-house, and it is some distance from the road to the window. Besides, this refers to the Monday, and the crime was done upon the Wednesday.

"On the Tuesday Peter Carey was in one of his blackest moods, flushed with drink and as savage as a dangerous wild beast. He roamed about the house, and the women ran for it when they heard him coming. Late in the evening he went down to his own hut. About two o'clock the following morning his daughter, who slept with her window open, heard a most fearful yell from that direction, but it was no unusual thing for him to bawl and shout when he was in drink, so no notice was taken. On rising at seven one of the maids noticed that the door of the hut was open, but so great was the terror which the man caused that it was midday before anyone would venture down to see what had become of him. Peeping into the open door they saw a sight which sent them flying with white faces into the village. Within an hour I was on the spot and had taken over the case.

"Well, I have fairly steady nerves, as you know, Mr Holmes, but I give you my word that I got a shake when I put my head into that little house. It was droning like a harmonium with the flies and bluebottles, and the floor and walls were like a slaughter-house. He had called it a cabin, and a cabin it was sure enough, for you would have thought that you were in a ship. There was a bunk at one end, a sea-chest, maps and charts, a picture of the SEA UNICORN, a line of log-books on a shelf, all exactly as one would expect to find it in a captain's room. And there in the middle of it was the man himself, his face twisted like a lost soul in torment, and his great brindled beard stuck upwards in his agony. Right through his broad breast a steel harpoon had been driven, and it had sunk deep into the wood of the wall behind him. He was pinned like a beetle on a card. Of course, he was quite dead, and had been so from the instant that he had uttered that last yell of agony.

"I know your methods, sir, and I applied them. Before I permitted anything to be moved I examined most carefully the ground outside, and also the floor of the room. There were no footmarks."

"Meaning that you saw none?"

"I assure you, sir, that there were none."

"My good Hopkins, I have investigated many crimes, but I have never yet seen one which was committed by a flying creature. As long as the criminal remains upon two legs so long must there be some indentation, some abrasion, some trifling displacement which can be detected by the scientific searcher. It is incredible that this blood-bespattered room contained no trace which could have aided us. I understand, however, from the inquest that there were some objects which you failed to overlook?"

The young inspector winced at my companion's ironical comments.

"I was a fool not to call you in at the time, Mr Holmes. However, that's past praying for now. Yes, there were several objects in the room which called for special attention. One was the harpoon with which the deed was committed. It had been snatched down from a rack on the wall. Two others remained there, and there was a vacant place for the third. On the stock was engraved 'S.S.. SEA UNICORN, Dundee.' This seemed to establish that the crime had been done in a moment of fury, and that the murderer had seized the first weapon which came in his way. The fact that the crime was committed at two in the morning, and yet Peter Carey was fully dressed, suggested that he had an appointment with the murderer, which is borne out by the fact that a bottle of rum and two dirty glasses stood upon the table."

"Yes," said Holmes; "I think that both inferences are permissible. Was there any other spirit but rum in the room?"

"Yes; there was a tantalus containing brandy and whisky on the sea-chest. It is of no importance to us, however, since the decanters were full, and it had therefore not been used."

"For all that its presence has some significance," said Holmes. "However, let us hear some more about the objects which do seem to you to bear upon the case."

"There was this tobacco-pouch upon the table."

"What part of the table?"

"It lay in the middle. It was of coarse seal-skin—the straight-haired skin, with a leather thong to bind it. Inside was 'P.C.' on the flap. There was half an ounce of strong ship's tobacco in it."

"Excellent! What more?"

Stanley Hopkins drew from his pocket a drab-covered note-book. The outside was rough and worn, the leaves discoloured. On the first page were written the initials "J. H. N." and the date "1883." Holmes laid it on the table and examined it in his minute way, while Hopkins and I gazed over each shoulder. On the second page were the printed letters "C. P. R.," and then came several sheets of numbers. Another heading was Argentine, another Costa Rica, and another San Paulo, each with pages of signs and figures after it.

"What do you make of these?" asked Holmes.

"They appear to be lists of Stock Exchange securities. I thought that 'J. H. N.' were the initials of a broker, and that 'C. P. R.' may have been his client."

"Try Canadian Pacific Railway," said Holmes.

Stanley Hopkins swore between his teeth and struck his thigh with his clenched hand.

"What a fool I have been!" he cried. "Of course, it is as you say. Then 'J. H. N.' are the only initials we have to solve.

I have already examined the old Stock Exchange lists, and I can find no one in 1883 either in the House or among the outside brokers whose initials correspond with these. Yet I feel that the clue is the most important one that I hold. You will admit, Mr Holmes, that there is a possibility that these initials are those of the second person who was present—in other words, of the murderer. I would also urge that the introduction into the case of a document relating to large masses of valuable securities gives us for the first time some indication of a motive for the crime."

Sherlock Holmes's face showed that he was thoroughly taken aback by this new development.

"I must admit both your points," said he. "I confess that this note-book, which did not appear at the inquest, modifies any views which I may have formed. I had come to a theory of the crime in which I can find no place for this. Have you endeavoured to trace any of the securities here mentioned?"

"Inquiries are now being made at the offices, but I fear that the complete register of the stockholders of these South American concerns is in South America, and that some weeks must elapse before we can trace the shares."

Holmes had been examining the cover of the note-book with his magnifying lens.

"Surely there is some discolouration here," said he.

"Yes, sir, it is a blood-stain. I told you that I picked the book off the floor."

"Was the blood-stain above or below?"

"On the side next to the boards."

"Which proves, of course, that the book was dropped after the crime was committed."

"Exactly, Mr Holmes. I appreciated that point, and I conjectured that it was dropped by the murderer in his hurried flight. It lay near the door."

"I suppose that none of these securities have been found among the property of the dead man?"

"No, sir."

"Have you any reason to suspect robbery?"

"No, sir. Nothing seemed to have been touched."

"Dear me, it is certainly a very interesting case. Then there was a knife, was there not?"

"A sheath-knife, still in its sheath. It lay at the feet of the dead man. Mrs Carey has identified it as being her husband's property."

Holmes was lost in thought for some time.

"Well," said he, at last, "I suppose I shall have to come out and have a look at it."

Stanley Hopkins gave a cry of joy.

"Thank you, sir. That will indeed be a weight off my mind."

Holmes shook his finger at the inspector.

"It would have been an easier task a week ago," said he. "But even now my visit may not be entirely fruitless. Watson, if you can spare the time I should be very glad of your company. If you will call a four-wheeler, Hopkins, we shall be ready to start for Forest Row in a quarter of an hour."

Alighting at the small wayside station, we drove for some miles through the remains of widespread woods, which were once part of that great forest which for so long held the Saxon invaders at bay—the impenetrable "weald," for sixty years the bulwark of Britain. Vast sections of it have been cleared, for this is the seat of the first iron-works of the country, and the trees have been felled to smelt the ore. Now the richer fields of the North have absorbed the trade, and nothing save these ravaged groves and great scars in the earth show the work of the past. Here in a clearing upon the green slope of a hill stood a long, low stone house, approached by a curving drive running through the fields. Nearer the road, and surrounded on three sides by bushes, was a small outhouse, one window and the door facing in our direction. It was the scene of the murder!

Stanley Hopkins led us first to the house, where he introduced us to a haggard, grey-haired woman, the widow of the murdered man, whose gaunt and deep-lined face, with the furtive look of terror in the depths of her red-rimmed eyes, told of the years of hardship and ill-usage which she had endured. With her was her daughter, a pale, fair-haired girl, whose eyes blazed defiantly at us as she told us that she was glad that her father was dead, and that she blessed the hand which had struck him down. It was a terrible household that Black Peter Carey had made for himself, and it was with a sense of relief that we found ourselves in the sunlight again and making our way along a path which had been worn across the fields by the feet of the dead man.

The outhouse was the simplest of dwellings, wooden-walled, shingle-roofed, one window beside the door and one on the farther side. Stanley Hopkins drew the key from his pocket, and had stooped to the lock, when he paused with a look of attention and surprise upon his face.

"Someone has been tampering with it," he said.

There could be no doubt of the fact. The woodwork was cut and the scratches showed white through the paint, as if they had been that instant done. Holmes had been examining the window.

"Someone has tried to force this also. Whoever it was has failed to make his way in. He must have been a very poor burglar."

"This is a most extraordinary thing," said the inspector; "I could swear that these marks were not here yesterday evening."

"Some curious person from the village, perhaps," I suggested.

"Very unlikely. Few of them would dare to set foot in the grounds, far less try to force their way into the cabin. What do you think of it, Mr Holmes?"

"I think that fortune is very kind to us."

"You mean that the person will come again?"

"It is very probable. He came expecting to find the door open. He tried to get in with the blade of a very small penknife. He could not manage it. What would he do?"

"Come again next night with a more useful tool."

"So I should say. It will be our fault if we are not there to receive him. Meanwhile, let me see the inside of the cabin."

The traces of the tragedy had been removed, but the furniture within the little room still stood as it had been on the night of the crime. For two hours, with most intense concentration, Holmes examined every object in turn, but his face showed that his quest was not a successful one. Once only he paused in his patient investigation.

"Have you taken anything off this shelf, Hopkins?"

"No; I have moved nothing."

"Something has been taken. There is less dust in this corner of the shelf than elsewhere. It may have been a book lying on its side. It may have been a box. Well, well, I can do nothing more. Let us walk in these beautiful woods, Watson, and give a few hours to the birds and the flowers. We shall meet you here later, Hopkins, and see if we can come to closer quarters with the gentleman who has paid this visit in the night."

It was past eleven o'clock when we formed our little ambuscade. Hopkins was for leaving the door of the hut open, but Holmes was of the opinion that this would rouse the suspicions of the stranger. The lock was a perfectly simple one, and only a strong blade was needed to push it back. Holmes also suggested that we should wait, not inside the hut, but outside it among the bushes which grew round the farther window. In this way we should be able to watch our man if he struck a light, and see what his object was in this stealthy nocturnal visit.

It was a long and melancholy vigil, and yet brought with it something of the thrill which the hunter feels when he lies beside the water pool and waits for the coming of the thirsty beast of prey. What savage creature was it which might steal upon us out of the darkness? Was it a fierce tiger of crime, which could only be taken fighting hard with flashing fang and claw, or would it prove to be some skulking jackal, dangerous only to the weak and unguarded?

In absolute silence we crouched amongst the bushes, waiting for whatever might come. At first the steps of a few belated villagers, or the sound of voices from the village, lightened our vigil; but one by one these interruptions died away and an absolute stillness fell upon us, save for the chimes of the distant church, which told us of the progress of the night, and for the rustle and whisper of a fine rain falling amid the foliage which roofed us in.

Half-past two had chimed, and it was the darkest hour which precedes the dawn, when we all started as a low but sharp click came from the direction of the gate. Someone had entered the drive. Again there was a long silence, and I had begun to fear that it was a false alarm, when a stealthy step was heard upon the other side of the hut, and a moment later a metallic scraping and clinking. The man was trying to force the lock! This time his skill was greater or his tool was better, for there was a sudden snap and the creak of the hinges. Then a match was struck, and next instant the steady light from a candle filled the interior of the hut. Through the gauze curtain our eyes were all riveted upon the scene within.

The nocturnal visitor was a young man, frail and thin, with a black moustache which intensified the deadly pallor of his face. He could not have been much above twenty years of age. I have never seen any human being who appeared to be in such a pitiable fright, for his teeth were visibly chattering and he was shaking in every limb. He was dressed like a gentleman, in Norfolk jacket and knickerbockers, with a cloth cap upon his head. We watched him staring round with frightened eyes. Then he laid the candle-end upon the table and disappeared from our view into one of the corners. He returned with a large book, one of the log-books which formed a line upon the shelves. Leaning on the table he rapidly turned over the leaves of this volume until he came to the entry which he sought. Then, with an angry gesture of his clenched hand, he closed the book, replaced it in the corner, and put out the light. He had hardly turned to leave the hut when Hopkins's hand was on the fellow's collar, and I heard his loud gasp of terror as he understood that he was taken. The candle was re-lit, and there was our wretched captive shivering and cowering in the grasp of the detective. He sank down upon the sea-chest, and looked helplessly from one of us to the other.

"Now, my fine fellow," said Stanley Hopkins, "who are you, and what do you want here?"

The man pulled himself together and faced us with an effort at self-composure.

"You are detectives, I suppose?" said he. "You imagine I am connected with the death of Captain Peter Carey. I assure you that I am innocent."

"We'll see about that," said Hopkins. "First of all, what is your name?"

"It is John Hopley Neligan."

I saw Holmes and Hopkins exchange a quick glance.

"What are you doing here?"

"Can I speak confidentially?"

"No, certainly not."

"Why should I tell you?"

"If you have no answer it may go badly with you at the trial."

The young man winced.

"Well, I will tell you," he said. "Why should I not? And yet I hate to think of this old scandal gaining a new lease of life. Did you ever hear of Dawson and Neligan?"

I could see from Hopkins's face that he never had; but Holmes was keenly interested.

"You mean the West-country bankers," said he. "They failed for a million, ruined half the county families of Cornwall, and Neligan disappeared."

"Exactly. Neligan was my father."

At last we were getting something positive, and yet it seemed a long gap between an absconding banker and Captain Peter Carey pinned against the wall with one of his own harpoons. We all listened intently to the young man's words.

"It was my father who was really concerned. Dawson had retired. I was only ten years of age at the time, but I was old enough to feel the shame and horror of it all. It has always been said that my father stole all the securities and fled. It is not true. It was his belief that if he were given time in which to realize them all would be well and every creditor paid in full. He started in his little yacht for Norway just before the warrant was issued for his arrest. I can remember that last night when he bade farewell to my mother. He left us a list of the securities he was taking, and he swore that he would come back with his honour cleared, and that none who had trusted him would suffer. Well, no word was ever heard from him again. Both the yacht and he vanished utterly. We believed, my mother and I, that he and it, with the securities that he had
220

taken with him, were at the bottom of the sea. We had a faithful friend, however, who is a business man, and it was he who discovered some time ago that some of the securities which my father had with him have reappeared on the London market. You can imagine our amazement. I spent months in trying to trace them, and at last, after many doublings and difficulties, I discovered that the original seller had been Captain Peter Carey, the owner of this hut.

"Naturally, I made some inquiries about the man. I found that he had been in command of a whaler which was due to return from the Arctic seas at the very time when my father was crossing to Norway. The autumn of that year was a stormy one, and there was a long succession of southerly gales. My father's yacht may well have been blown to the north, and there met by Captain Peter Carey's ship. If that were so, what had become of my father? In any case, if I could prove from Peter Carey's evidence how these securities came on the market it would be a proof that my father had not sold them, and that he had no view to personal profit when he took them.

"I came down to Sussex with the intention of seeing the captain, but it was at this moment that his terrible death occurred. I read at the inquest a description of his cabin, in which it stated that the old log-books of his vessel were preserved in it. It struck me that if I could see what occurred in the month of August 1883, on board the SEA UNICORN, I might settle the mystery of my father's fate. I tried last night to get at these log-books, but was unable to open the door. To-night I tried again, and succeeded; but I find that the pages which deal with that month have been torn from the book. It was at that moment I found myself a prisoner in your hands."

"Is that all?" asked Hopkins.

"Yes, that is all." His eyes shifted as he said it.

"You have nothing else to tell us?"

He hesitated.

"No; there is nothing."

"You have not been here before last night?"

"No."

"Then how do you account for THAT?" cried Hopkins, as he held up the damning note-book, with the initials of our prisoner on the first leaf and the blood-stain on the cover.

The wretched man collapsed. He sank his face in his hands and trembled all over.

"Where did you get it?" he groaned. "I did not know. I thought I had lost it at the hotel."

"That is enough," said Hopkins, sternly. "Whatever else you have to say you must say in court. You will walk down with me now to the police-station. Well, Mr Holmes, I am very much obliged to you and to your friend for coming down to help me. As it turns out your presence was unnecessary, and I would have brought the case to this successful issue without you; but none the less I am very grateful. Rooms have been reserved for you at the Brambletye Hotel, so we can all walk down to the village together."

"Well, Watson, what do you think of it?" asked Holmes, as we travelled back next morning.

"I can see that you are not satisfied."

"Oh, yes, my dear Watson, I am perfectly satisfied. At the same time Stanley Hopkins's methods do not commend themselves to me. I am disappointed in Stanley Hopkins. I had hoped for better things from him. One should always look for a possible alternative and provide against it. It is the first rule of criminal investigation."

"What, then, is the alternative?"

"The line of investigation which I have myself been pursuing. It may give us nothing. I cannot tell. But at least I shall follow it to the end."

Several letters were waiting for Holmes at Baker Street. He snatched one of them up, opened it, and burst out into a triumphant chuckle of laughter.

"Excellent, Watson. The alternative develops. Have you telegraph forms? Just write a couple of messages for me: 'Sumner, Shipping Agent, Ratcliff Highway. Send three men on, to arrive ten to-morrow morning.—Basil.' That's my name in those parts. The other is: 'Inspector Stanley Hopkins, 46, Lord Street, Brixton. Come breakfast to-morrow at nine-thirty. Important. Wire if unable to come.—Sherlock Holmes.' There, Watson, this infernal case has haunted me for ten days. I hereby banish it completely from my presence. To-morrow I trust that we shall hear the last of it for ever."

Sharp at the hour named Inspector Stanley Hopkins appeared, and we sat down together to the excellent breakfast which Mrs Hudson had prepared. The young detective was in high spirits at his success.

"You really think that your solution must be correct?" asked Holmes.

"I could not imagine a more complete case."

"It did not seem to me conclusive."

"You astonish me, Mr Holmes. What more could one ask for?"

"Does your explanation cover every point?"

"Undoubtedly. I find that young Neligan arrived at the Brambletye Hotel on the very day of the crime. He came on the pretence of playing golf. His room was on the ground-floor, and he could get out when he liked. That very night he went down to Woodman's Lee, saw Peter Carey at the hut, quarrelled with him, and killed him with the harpoon. Then, horrified by what he had done, he fled out of the hut, dropping the note-book which he had brought with him in order to question Peter Carey about these different securities. You may have observed that some of them were marked with ticks, and the others—the great majority—were not. Those which are ticked have been traced on the London market; but the others presumably were still in the possession of Carey, and young Neligan, according to his own account, was anxious to recover them in order to do the right thing by his father's creditors. After his flight he did not dare to approach the hut again for some time; but at last he forced himself to do so in order to obtain the information which he needed. Surely that is all simple and obvious?"

Holmes smiled and shook his head.

"It seems to me to have only one drawback, Hopkins, and that is that it is intrinsically impossible. Have you tried to drive a harpoon through a body? No? Tut, tut, my dear sir, you must really pay attention to these details. My friend Watson could tell you that I spent a whole morning in that exercise. It is no easy matter, and requires a strong and practised arm. But this blow was delivered with such violence that the head of the weapon sank deep into the wall. Do you imagine that this anaemic youth was capable of so frightful an assault? Is he the man who hobnobbed in rum and water with Black Peter in the dead of the night? Was it his profile that was seen on the blind two nights before? No, no, Hopkins; it is another and a more formidable person for whom we must seek."

The detective's face had grown longer and longer during Holmes's speech. His hopes and his ambitions were all crumbling about him. But he would not abandon his position without a struggle.

"You can't deny that Neligan was present that night, Mr Holmes. The book will prove that. I fancy that I have evidence enough to satisfy a jury, even if you are able to pick a hole in it. Besides, Mr Holmes, I have laid my hand upon MY man. As to this terrible person of yours, where is he?"

"I rather fancy that he is on the stair," said Holmes, serenely. "I think, Watson, that you would do well to put that revolver where you can reach it." He rose, and laid a written paper upon a side-table. "Now we are ready," said he.

There had been some talking in gruff voices outside, and now Mrs Hudson opened the door to say that there were three men inquiring for Captain Basil.

"Show them in one by one," said Holmes.

The first who entered was a little ribston-pippin of a man, with ruddy cheeks and fluffy white side-whiskers. Holmes had drawn a letter from his pocket.

"What name?" he asked.

"James Lancaster."

"I am sorry, Lancaster, but the berth is full. Here is half a sovereign for your trouble. Just step into this room and wait there for a few minutes."

The second man was a long, dried-up creature, with lank hair and sallow cheeks. His name was Hugh Pattins. He also received his dismissal, his half-sovereign, and the order to wait.

The third applicant was a man of remarkable appearance. A fierce bull-dog face was framed in a tangle of hair and beard, and two bold dark eyes gleamed behind the cover of thick, tufted, overhung eyebrows. He saluted and stood sailor-fashion, turning his cap round in his hands.

"Your name?" asked Holmes.

"Patrick Cairns."

"Harpooner?"

"Yes, sir. Twenty-six voyages."

"Dundee, I suppose?"

"Yes, sir."

"And ready to start with an exploring ship?"

"Yes, sir."

"What wages?"

"Eight pounds a month."

"Could you start at once?"

"As soon as I get my kit."

"Have you your papers?"

"Yes, sir." He took a sheaf of worn and greasy forms from his pocket. Holmes glanced over them and returned them.

"You are just the man I want," said he. "Here's the agreement on the side-table. If you sign it the whole matter will be settled."

The seaman lurched across the room and took up the pen.

"Shall I sign here?" he asked, stooping over the table.

Holmes leaned over his shoulder and passed both hands over his neck.

"This will do," said he.

I heard a click of steel and a bellow like an enraged bull. The next instant Holmes and the seaman were rolling on the ground together. He was a man of such gigantic strength that, even with the handcuffs which Holmes had so deftly fastened upon his wrists, he would have very quickly overpowered my friend had Hopkins and I not rushed to his rescue. Only when I pressed the cold muzzle of the revolver to his temple did he at last understand that resistance was vain. We lashed his ankles with cord and rose breathless from the struggle.

"I must really apologize, Hopkins," said Sherlock Holmes; "I fear that the scrambled eggs are cold. However, you will enjoy the rest of your breakfast all the better, will you not, for the thought that you have brought your case to a triumphant conclusion."

Stanley Hopkins was speechless with amazement.

"I don't know what to say, Mr Holmes," he blurted out at last, with a very red face. "It seems to me that I have been making a fool of myself from the beginning. I understand now, what I should never have forgotten, that I am the pupil and you are the master. Even now I see what you have done, but I don't know how you did it, or what it signifies."

"Well, well," said Holmes, good-humouredly. "We all learn by experience, and your lesson this time is that you should never lose sight of the alternative. You were so absorbed in young Neligan that you could not spare a thought to Patrick Cairns, the true murderer of Peter Carey."

The hoarse voice of the seaman broke in on our conversation.

"See here, mister," said he, "I make no complaint of being man-handled in this fashion, but I would have you call things by their right names. You say I murdered Peter Carey; I say I KILLED Peter Carey, and there's all the difference. Maybe you don't believe what I say. Maybe you think I am just slinging you a yarn."

"Not at all," said Holmes. "Let us hear what you have to say."

"It's soon told, and, by the Lord, every word of it is truth. I knew Black Peter, and when he pulled out his knife I whipped a harpoon through him sharp, for I knew that it was him or me. That's how he died. You can call it murder. Anyhow, I'd as soon die with a rope round my neck as with Black Peter's knife in my heart."

"How came you there?" asked Holmes.

"I'll tell it you from the beginning. Just sit me up a little so as I can speak easy. It was in '83 that it happened— August of that year. Peter Carey was master of the SEA UNICORN, and I was spare harpooner. We were coming out of the ice-pack on our way home, with head winds and a week's southerly gale, when we picked up a little craft that had been blown north. There was one man on her—a landsman. The crew had thought she would founder, and had made for the

Norwegian coast in the dinghy. I guess they were all drowned. Well, we took him on board, this man, and he and the skipper had some long talks in the cabin. All the baggage we took off with him was one tin box. So far as I know, the man's name was never mentioned, and on the second night he disappeared as if he had never been. It was given out that he had either thrown himself overboard or fallen overboard in the heavy weather that we were having. Only one man knew what had happened to him, and that was me, for with my own eyes I saw the skipper tip up his heels and put him over the rail in the middle watch of a dark night, two days before we sighted the Shetland lights.

"Well, I kept my knowledge to myself and waited to see what would come of it. When we got back to Scotland it was easily hushed up, and nobody asked any questions. A stranger died by an accident, and it was nobody's business to inquire. Shortly after Peter Carey gave up the sea, and it was long years before I could find where he was. I guessed that he had done the deed for the sake of what was in that tin box, and that he could afford now to pay me well for keeping my mouth shut.

"I found out where he was through a sailor man that had met him in London, and down I went to squeeze him. The first night he was reasonable enough, and was ready to give me what would make me free of the sea for life. We were to fix it all two nights later. When I came I found him three parts drunk and in a vile temper. We sat down and we drank and we yarned about old times, but the more he drank the less I liked the look on his face. I spotted that harpoon upon the wall, and I thought I might need it before I was through. Then at last he broke out at me, spitting and cursing, with murder in his eyes and a great clasp-knife in his hand. He had not time to get it from the sheath before I had the harpoon through him. Heavens! what a yell he gave; and his face gets between me and my sleep! I stood there, with his blood splashing round me, and I waited for a bit; but all was quiet, so I took heart once more. I looked round, and there was the tin box on a shelf. I had as much right to it as Peter Carey, anyhow, so I took it with me and left the hut. Like a fool I left my baccy-pouch upon the table.

"Now I'll tell you the queerest part of the whole story. I had hardly got outside the hut when I heard someone coming, and I hid among the bushes. A man came slinking along, went into the hut, gave a cry as if he had seen a ghost, and legged it as hard as he could run until he was out of sight. Who he was or what he wanted is more than I can tell. For my part I walked ten miles, got a train at Tunbridge Wells, and so reached London, and no one the wiser.

"Well, when I came to examine the box I found there was no money in it, and nothing but papers that I would not dare to sell. I had lost my hold on Black Peter, and was stranded in London without a shilling. There was only my trade left. I saw these advertisements about harpooners and high wages, so I went to the shipping agents, and they sent me here. That's all I know, and I say again that if I killed Black Peter the law should give me thanks, for I saved them the price of a hempen rope."

"A very clear statement," said Holmes, rising and lighting his pipe. "I think, Hopkins, that you should lose no time in conveying your prisoner to a place of safety. This room is not well adapted for a cell, and Mr Patrick Cairns occupies too large a proportion of our carpet."

"Mr Holmes," said Hopkins, "I do not know how to express my gratitude. Even now I do not understand how you attained this result."

"Simply by having the good fortune to get the right clue from the beginning. It is very possible if I had known about this note-book it might have led away my thoughts, as it did yours. But all I heard pointed in the one direction. The amazing strength, the skill in the use of the harpoon, the rum and water, the seal-skin tobacco-pouch, with the coarse tobacco— all these pointed to a seaman, and one who had been a whaler. I was convinced that the initials 'P.C.' upon the pouch were a coincidence, and not those of Peter Carey, since he seldom smoked, and no pipe was found in his cabin. You remember that I asked whether whisky and brandy were in the cabin. You said they were. How many landsmen are there who would drink rum when they could get these other spirits? Yes, I was certain it was a seaman."

"And how did you find him?"

"My dear sir, the problem had become a very simple one. If it were a seaman, it could only be a seaman who had been with him on the SEA UNICORN. So far as I could learn he had sailed in no other ship. I spent three days in wiring to Dundee, and at the end of that time I had ascertained the names of the crew of the SEA UNICORN in 1883. When I found Patrick Cairns among the harpooners my research was nearing its end. I argued that the man was probably in London, and that he would desire to leave the country for a time. I therefore spent some days in the East-end, devised an Arctic expedition, put forth tempting terms for harpooners who would serve under Captain Basil—and behold the result!"

"Wonderful!" cried Hopkins. "Wonderful!"

"You must obtain the release of young Neligan as soon as possible," said Holmes. "I confess that I think you owe him some apology. The tin box must be returned to him, but, of course, the securities which Peter Carey has sold are lost for ever. There's the cab, Hopkins, and you can remove your man. If you want me for the trial, my address and that of Watson will be somewhere in Norway— I'll send particulars later."

"The Adventure Of Silver Blaze" Sidney Paget.

Acknowledgements

"I must thank you for it all. I might not have gone but for you, and so have missed the finest study I ever came across." *A Study in Scarlet.*

Thank you MX, Sherlock Holmes Books, for giving me the chance of a lifetime, and David Marcum for the New Sherlock Holmes story anthologies. The Belanger Brothers always tantalising short story invitations led to some of my best. Mystery Magazine, who published my first pulp fiction story, a long-held writer's dream.

The ACD Society for choosing my short story "Sir Arthur and the Time Machine" as one of their first Doylian Fiction Award winners.

The marvellous narrator of my mystery's, J.T. McDaniel, whose portrayals are splendid. If you'd like to hear Doctor Watson read my book, visit your favourite audiobook supplier.

Thank you, Steve and MX. It is wonderful to be a part of Sherlock Holmes Books and so happy to be grouped with such wonderfully imaginative murder and mayhem authors! Ever so grateful. With Sherlock Holmes mysteries, you get all the terror and suspense of the others, yet scientifically solved with true justice in the end.

Awan, the talented artist who designed the smashing cover for this book. I am grateful for your effortless collaboration, keen design and illustration skills, and especially for putting Sherlock Holmes on the cover.

I want to thank my friends and family for their kindness and patience. You have taught me so much and I am learning as fast as I can how to be properly grateful for all the big and little aspects of life, for those, met and not yet met, for joys shared and those whose leaving brings us together again.

Thank you, friends of Jeremy I met in Clapham Park, London. Maureen Whittaker for bringing me into the great research adventure that became her book, *Jeremy Brett, Playing a Part*. Friends and family who have been with me through this literary rollercoaster ride: Julia Altabef, Pamela Ann Russo, Robert Sturgeon, Frank Bruszkiewicz, Gary and Jennifer Culp, Ann and Will Keech, Paula Clinchy, Nieves Fernandez, and Sue Davis. Sincere thanks go to my accomplished author community: Roger Johnson, Catherine Cooke, Christine Bush, Mattias Boström, Jayantika Ganguly, Wendy Heyman-Marsaw, Craig Stephen Copland, Gary Culp, Harry DeMaio, Geri Schear, Margaret Walsh, Orlando Pearson, Petr Kopl, Paul Thomas Miller, and Linda Pritchard. And to all the welcoming Sherlockian, Holmesian, Doylian, and Watsonian communities and their wonderful journals that give writers the chance to publish and be read by like-minded folk. I am a member of: The Sherlock Holmes Society of London, The Adventuresses of Sherlock Holmes, The ACD Society, The John H. Watson Society, and The Sherlock Holmes Society of India, plus my superb and environmentally friendly artist collective, the Philadelphia Dumpster Divers.

I am supremely grateful to Sir Arthur Conan Doyle. His literature and his dynamic spirit are my best inspiration. For bringing Sherlock Holmes to life, and for his literary sidekick, Doctor John H. Watson, a published author, doctor, soldier, an honourable gentleman, and a crack shot. He is one half of the greatest friendship in English literature.

Frederic Dorr Steele. The Mazarin Stone. "The one thing I don't know about it, you're going to tell me now." Holmes announced calmly.

Notes For Curious
Instead of Footnotes

Works Used Throughout (Chapter Notes Follow)

1. Doyle, Sir Arthur Conan. *The Complete Sherlock Holmes. Volume I and II.* Doubleday, New York, US. 1905, 1917,1927, 1930.
2. Doyle, Sir Arthur Conan. *The Original Illustrated 'Strand' Sherlock Holmes.* Wordsworth Editions, Hertfordshire, UK. 1989.
3. Baring-Gold, William. *Sherlock Holmes of Baker Street: A Life of the World's First Consulting Detective.* Calabash Press, British Columbia, Canada. 1962.
4. Baring-Gold, William. *The Annotated Sherlock Holmes.* Clarkson N. Potter, New York. 1967.
5. Klinger, Leslie. *New Annotated Sherlock Holmes.* New York: W. W. Norton & Company, 2005.
6. *Bradshaw's Handbook 1861.* London: HarperCollins, 2014 (originally published as *Bradshaw's Descriptive Railway Hand-Book of Great Britain and Ireland.* 1861.)
7. *Bradshaw's Monthly Continental Railway, Steam Transit, and. General Guide 1887* - Google Books. https://books.google.com/books?id=w3dKAAAAYAAJ&vq=calais&pg=PP1#v=onepage&q&f=false
8. Doyle, Sir Arthur Conan. *Memories and Adventures.* London: Hodder & Stoughton Ltd. 1924. The copyright for this publication is in the public domain.
9. Liebow, Ely M. *Doctor Joe Bell, Model for Sherlock Holmes.* Madison, Wisconsin: Popular Press, 2007.
10. "The Arthur Conan Doyle Encyclopaedia." Alexis Barquin. https://www.arthur-conan-doyle.com/index.php/
11. BHO British History Online. IHR Institute of Historical Research, School of Advanced Study, University of London. https://www.british-history.ac.uk/

11. National Library of Scotland, Georeferenced maps, London, 1893-6. I spend delightful hours in research here. https://maps.nls.uk/geo/find/#zoom=16&lat=51.50349&lon=-0.13541&layers=38&b=1&z=1&point=0,0.

12. Altabef, Gretchen. *Sherlock Holmes These Scattered Houses*. MX Publishing, Sherlock Holmes Books, London, UK. 2019.

13. Altabef, Gretchen. *Sherlock Holmes A Remarkable Power of Stimulus*. MX Publishing, Sherlock Holmes Books, London, UK. 2020.

14. Altabef, Gretchen. *Sherlock Holmes The Keys of Death*. MX Publishing, Sherlock Holmes Books, London, UK. 2021.

15. Altabef, Gretchen. *Sherlock Holmes Five Miles Of Country*. MX Publishing, Sherlock Holmes Books, London, UK. 2024.

NOTE 1: Sir Arthur Conan Doyle wrote 60 Sherlock Holmes stories, including 4 novels. He was a prolific author of 1,874 works. He wrote over 300 pieces of fiction (including 24 novels) of all genres: history, fantasy, drama, adventure, science-fiction, crime, war. Plus over 1500 other works as essays, plays, poems, articles, letters to the press, pamphlets, and interviews on every subject such as politics, religion, war, medicine, crime, injustice, etc.

Introduction

1. Steele, Fredrick Dorr. Arthur Conan Doyle. "The Blanched Soldier." *Liberty Magazine*, New York, US. 1926.

2. Doyle, Arthur Conan. Sherlock Holmes - The Complete Long Stories. Preface. First collection of the four Sherlock Holmes novels written between 1887 and 1914. John Murray, UK, 1929.

3. Doyle, Arthur Conan. *Memories And Adventures*. Autobiography. *The Strand Magazine* October 1923 to July 1924. Hodder & Stoughton Ltd, London, UK. 1924.

4. Blathwayt, Raymond. "A Talk with Dr. Conan Doyle" An interview of Arthur Conan Doyle. *The Bookman* (vol. 2 #8 p. 50-51) in May 1892.

5. Hutchisson, James M. *Ernest Hemingway A New Life.* Penn State University Press, Philadelphia, US. 2017.

6. Blathwayt, Raymond. "A Talk with Dr. Conan Doyle" An interview of Arthur Conan Doyle. *The Bookman* (vol. 2 #8 p. 50-51) in May 1892.

7. King, Stephen. *On Writing. A Memoir of the Craft.* Scribner, New York, US. 2020.

8. Jekyll, Gertrude; Weaver, Lawrence. "Gardens for Small Country Houses" *Country Life Magazine.* 1912.

9. Doyle, Arthur Conan. "A Gaudy Death: Conan Doyle tells the True Story of Sherlock Holmes." *Tit-Bits.* 15 December 1900.

10. Wills, George Roland. *A Short Phantasy. Jeremy Brett meets Mr. Sherlock Holmes.* Confederate Publishing. 2011.

11. Doyle, Arthur Conan. *Sherlock Holmes - The Complete Long Stories.* Preface. First collection of the four Sherlock Holmes novels written between 1887 and 1914. John Murray, UK, 1929.

NOTE 2: The casting of Doctor Watson as the author of the Sherlock Holmes stories was based upon the beginning words of the first Sherlock Holmes story, *A Study in Scarlet. "Being a Reprint from the Reminiscences of John H. Watson, M.D. late of the Army Medical Department. "* This and other references throughout the canon placed Doctor Watson firmly in position as the chronicler of the life and work of the great detective, Mr Sherlock Holmes. "The Game" follows and was half-humorously acknowledged by all members of the worldwide Sherlock Holmes Literary Societies. It states that Sherlock Holmes and Doctor John H. Watson lived. That everyone mentioned in these chronicles were real persons. Many believe they may even be alive today. I think mostly because of his and his progeny's animosity towards these societies, Sir Arthur Conan Doyle was relegated to the role of Watson's literary agent. But don't quote me on that.

Boxing Day Brother Mine

1. Paget, Sidney. (1894.) Gillette, William. (1916.) "Mycroft and Sherlock Holmes." (By G. Altabef.) Arthur Conan Doyle. "The Adventure of the Bruce Partington Plans." *The Strand Magazine,* London, UK. Friends of Gillette Castle State Park. www.gillettecastlefriends.org/

2. Connelly, Mark. "A Brief History of Boxing Day" *History Extra. BBC History Magazine* and *BBC History Revealed.* Dec. 26, 2022. www.historyextra.com/period/victorian/brief-history-boxing-day-christmas-traditions/

3. The Editors of Encyclopaedia Britannica. "Boxing Day." *Encyclopaedia Britannica,* May 25, 2024. www.britannica.com/topic/Boxing-Day/

4. New World Encyclopedia. "Boxing Day." Nov. 20, 2023. www.newworldencyclopedia.org/p/index.php?title=Boxing_Day&oldid=1128192/

5. Qaiser, S. Pervez. "The legacy of Boxing Day Tests - Cricket's grandest year-end spectacle." *Hindustan Times,* Dec. 26, 2017.

6. "Christmas-box." OED Online, 1st ed. Oxford University Press. 1889.

7. Brown, Cameron. "Christmas Facts, Figures & Fun." *Facts, Figures & Fun.* 2006. ISBN 978-1904332275/

8. Altabef, Gretchen. "Boxing Day Brother Mine." First published in *The MX Book of New Sherlock Holmes.* Part XLIII: 2024 Annual (1874-1888.) Edited by David Marcum.

In The Land of The Living

1. Steele, Frederick Dorr. "The Return of Sherlock Holmes." Arthur Conan Doyle. "The Adventure of the Empty House." Cover. *Collier's Weekly Magazine,* New York, US, 1903.

2. Sir Arthur Conan Doyle said much the same thing in December 1894. "An Alpine Pass on Ski." *The Strand, McClure's, The Philadelphia Inquirer,* et al.

3. The 13th Dalai Lama, Thubten Gyatso, led his beloved Tibet from 1895 to 1933. Both the British and the Chinese invaded his country. He fled with the help of Agvan Dorzhiev to India for safety. China deposed him, but he rejected their jurisdiction and returned to create an independent and more democratic Tibet. He was the first Dalai Lama to bring his country out of isolation and into the world.

4. Historic Ensemble of the Potala Palace, Lhasa. *UNESCO World Heritage List.* https://whc.unesco.org/en/list/707

5. Laird, Thomas. *The Story of Tibet: Conversations with the Dalai Lama.* Grove Press, New York. 2006.

6. *Tibetan Monks and Lamas.* "Buddha's Fire Sermon." http://factsanddetails.com/china/cat6/sub34/item218.html

7. Altabef, Gretchen. "In The Land Of The Living." *Mystery Magazine*, Ontario, Canada. Published October 2021.

NOTE 3: Though one could say there were many Lamas in Tibet at this time, the Dalai Lama would be considered the "head Llama." As Watson mentioned in, "The Adventure of the Empty House." Most likely, he was unsure of the exact title. Certainly, he had forgotten how to spell it. After all, I did not meet with a long-necked animal in the Andes of South America. Possibly, I was unreachable at the time, or he was hurrying to make his *Strand* deadline. The title, Dalai Lama means "Ocean of Wisdom."

Sir Arthur & The Time Machine

1. Robida, Albert. *The Future Imagined.* La Vie Électrique. Image created for the Paris 1900 World Exposition. 1890.

2. Altabef, Gretchen. "Sir Arthur & The Time Machine." *Sherlock Holmes Further Adventures in the Realms of H. G. Wells*. Belanger Books. Manchester, NH, 2022.

3. Reynolds, Sheldon. *Sherlock Holmes and Doctor Watson*. Polish/British TV Production. Geoffrey Whitehead, Donald Pickering, Patrick Newell. 1979/1980.

4. The Mysterious Bookshop is presently located at 58 Warren Street, New York, N.Y. 10007. In Tribeca, just south of Greenwich Village.

5. Otto Penzler, the creator of *American Mystery Classics*, is also the founder of the *Mysterious Press* (1975); Mysterious Press.com (2011), an electronic-book publishing company; and New York City's Mysterious Bookshop (1979). He has won a Raven, the Ellery Queen Award, two Edgars (for the *Encyclopedia of Mystery and Detection*, 1977, and *The Lineup*, 2010), and lifetime achievement awards from *Noircon* and *The Strand Magazine*. He has edited over 70 anthologies and written extensively about mystery fiction.

6. Giovanni, Paul. *The Crucifer of Blood*. Samuel French, Inc. 1978. Jeremy Brett portrayed Doctor Watson at the Ahmanson Theatre in Los Angeles, 1980. Four years before Mr Brett redefined Sherlock Holmes for Granada TV, Manchester, UK. 1984–1994.

7. Doyle, Arthur Conan. *The Sign Of Four*. "When you have eliminated the impossible, whatever remains, however improbable, must be the truth." *Lippincott's Magazine*, Philadelphia, PA, US, Feb. 1890.

8. Thomas, Lewis M.D. "Vibes", *New England Journal of Medicine*, Jan. 13, 1972. 11th dean of NYU School of Medicine.

9. Doyle, Arthur Conan. "The Adventure of the Copper Beeches." *The Strand Magazine*, London, UK. 1892. "The pressure of public opinion can do in the town what the law cannot accomplish. There is no lane so vile that the scream of a tortured child, or the thud of a drunkard's blow, does not beget sympathy and indignation among

the neighbours, and then the whole machinery of justice is ever so close that a word of complaint can set it going, and there is but a step between the crime and the dock."

A Watsonian Conundrum

1. Steele, Frederick Dorr. "My Collection Of M's Is A Fine One." Illustration for *Collier's Weekly Magazine*. New York, US. 1903. Arthur Conan Doyle. "The Adventure of the Empty House."
2. Doyle, Arthur Conan. "The Field Bazaar" was published in The *Student*, a University of Edinburgh school magazine, UK. 20 November 1896.

NOTE 4: The Watsonian is the literary journal of the John H. Watson Society. They have been very good to this author, publishing my first piece, "I Want a Watson." "The John H. Watson Society seeks a level of equality in scholarship and enthusiasm for the life and work of John H. Watson, M. D. We are an open and inclusive Society, seeking the collegiality and conviviality of members worldwide and at all stages of involvement in Watsonian, Sherlockian and Holmesian interests. Really, we are about having fun." www.johnhwatsonsociety.com/

NOTE 5: The Bazaar for which "The Field Bazaar" was written was held to raise funds for a pavilion and the equipment necessary for a 13-acre cricket field for the University of Edinburgh. Conan Doyle was an avid cricket player. *The Student Magazine* began its article with: "Dr. A. Conan Doyle, another of our graduates, has contributed an original story of the 'Sherlock Holmes' type. We all remember the indignation aroused by the death of the redoubtable detective, a few years ago. This is the only 'Sherlock Holmes' story published since then, and we have to offer our best thanks to the writer for his kindness in thus helping us and the Bazaar."

NOTE 6: Arthur Conan Doyle wrote 60 (or 62) original Sherlock Holmes stories. Everything else is pastiche: the marvellous stories he inspired us to create from our imaginations. No matter how we categorise pastiche, it is something else from the 60 (62) stories Doyle created. Therefore, it is through imagination and genius that we connect with Conan Doyle and Sherlock Holmes.

Miss Annie Harrison's Rose Soliloquy

1. Peters, Charles, editor of monograph: *A Crown of Flowers, being poems and pictures collected from the pages of The Girl's Own Paper.* "The Crown Rose." British Library digitised image shelfmark: "Digital Store 11602.gg.11." Religious Tract Society, London. 1883.

2. Doyle, Sir Arthur Conan. *The Original Illustrated 'Strand' Sherlock Holmes.* Wordsworth Editions, Hertfordshire, UK 1989.

3. "The Arthur Conan Doyle Encyclopaedia." Maintained by Alexis Barquin: www.arthur-conan-doyle.com/index.php/Sherlock_Holmes/

4. Chang, Elizabeth Hope. *Novel Cultivations: Plants in British Literature of the Global Nineteenth Century.* University of Virginia Press, 2019.

5. de Lorris, Guillaume; de Meun, Jean. "The Romance of the Rose." "Le Roman de la Rose" is a medieval poem, a notable instance of courtly literature, purporting to provide a "mirror of love" in which the whole art of romantic love is disclosed. Washington State University: https://public.wsu.edu/~delahoyd/medieval/rose.html/

6. Jay Finley Christ, *An Irregular Guide to Sherlock Holmes of Baker Street,* New York: Argus Books, 1947. www.arthur-conan-

doyle.com/index.php?title=Abbreviations_for_the_Sherlock_H
olmes_stories/

7. Unless otherwise noted, all quotes are from Sir Arthur Conan Doyle's, "The Adventure Of The Naval Treaty."

NOTE 7: According to Mr Baring-Gould, Doctor Watson places the action of "The Second Stain" in 1886, while the events of "The Naval Treaty" followed in the year 1889.

Mrs Hudson's Garden

1. Frankie, Gordon W; Thorp, Robbin W; Coville, Rollin E; Ertter, Barbara. *California Bees and Blooms.* Bee Anatomy Illustration. Heyday Books, Berkeley, CA, US. 2014.
2. Jekyll, Gertrude; Weaver, Lawrence. *Arts and Crafts Gardens.* First published as "Gardens for Small Country Houses" by *Country Life* Magazine. 1912. Antique Collectors' Club, Suffolk, UK. 2005.
3. Moore, Thomas. "A piece of sky and a chunk of earth lie lodged in the heart of every human being." Irish poet, songwriter, and singer, 1779-1852.
4. Doyle, Sir Arthur Conan. "The Adventure Of The Naval Treaty." *The Strand Magazine*, London, UK. 1893.
5. Altabef, Gretchen. First published in the novel, *The Keys Of Death.* MX Publishing Sherlock Holmes Books. London, UK. 2021.
6. William Shakespeare, 1564-1616.
7. Nathaniel Hawthorne, American author (The Scarlet Letter, etc.), 1804-1864.
8. Jekyll, Gertrude. *Home And Garden; Notes and thoughts, practical and critical, of a worker in both.* Longmans, Green and Co. London, New York, Bombay. 1900. "I plant rosemary all over the garden, so pleasant is it to know that at every few steps one may draw the kindly branchlets through one's hand, and have the enjoyment of their incomparable incense; and I grow it against walls, so that the sun may draw out its inexhaustible sweetness to greet me as I pass."

9. Hugh Miller, Scottish geologist, palaeontologist, and folklorist. "Life is itself a school, and Nature always a fresh study." 1802-1856.

10. William Blake, English poet and artist. "In seed-time learn, in harvest teach, in winter enjoy." 1757-1827.

11. Tull, Jethro. *The New Horse-Houghing Husbandry: Or An Essay on the Principles of Tillage and Vegetation.* Wherein Is Shewn, A Method Of Introducing A Sort Of Vineyard-Culture Into The Corn-Fields, In Order To Increase Their Product, And Diminish The Common Expense, By The Use Of Instruments Lately Invented. London, UK. 1731. Internet Archive: https://archive.org/details/bim_eighteenth-century_the-new-horse-houghing-h_tull-jethro_1731/page/n13/mode/2up/

12. Card, Adrian; Whiting, David; Wilson, Carl; Reeder, Jean, Ph.D.; Goldhamer, Dan. CMG Garden Notes #234 "Organic Fertilizers: Fish and Seaweed." *Master Gardener*, Colorado State University, Extension, 2015.

For further reference:

13. Krohn, Elise. "Creating Community Gardens Guidelines and Resources for Gardeners in the Pacific Northwest." Northwest Indian College, 2013.

14. Stout, Ruth. *How to Have a Green Thumb Without an Aching Back* and *Gardening Without Work.* Stout's techniques remain consistent with the "no-till" gardening methods soil experts recommend today. www.motherearthnews.com/

15. *Companion-Planting.* West Virginia University Extension: https://extension.wvu.edu/lawn-gardening-pests/gardening/garden-management/companion-planting#:~:text=Like%20people%2C%20some%20plants%20thrive,three%20rows%20of%20each%20other/

16. Fall/Winter Planting Suggestions: Burpee Seed Catalogue. www.burpee.com/

17. Natural Bug Repellents. *Great Garden Website*: http://www.no-dig-vegetablegarden.com/list-of-garden-pests.html/

18. Royal Horticultural Society. 80 Vincent Square, London, UK, SW1P 2PE. www.rhs.org.uk/about-us/what-we-do/our-history/

A Toast Darling

1. Steele, Frederick Dorr; Paget, Sidney; Altabef, G. Collage: "A Toast Darling." 2024. Arthur Conan Doyle's stories: "The Adventure of the Speckled Band." *The Strand Magazine*, London, UK. 1892. "The Adventure of the Golden Pince-Nez." *Collier's Weekly Magazine*, New York, US. 1904.

2. Doyle, Sir Arthur Conan. "The Adventure of the Dying Detective." *The Strand Magazine*, London, UK. 1913. Quote: "I give you my word that for three days I have tasted neither food nor drink until you were good enough to pour me out that glass of water. But it is the tobacco which I find most irksome."

3. Wills, George Roland. "A Short Phantasy." Jeremy Brett meets Mr. Sherlock Holmes. Amazon. Jan. 9, 1996. Written 4 months after Mr Brett's death. (Sept. 12, 1995.)

4. William Gillette. 1853-1937. American playwright and actor, Portrayed Sherlock Holmes for 35 years on stage and film. https://www.britannica.com/biography/William-Hooker-Gillette/

5. Ladinsky, Daniel. *The Gift*. A collection of the poetry of the 14th century Persian Sufi mystic, Haviz. Penguin Books, London, UK. 1999. Haviz poem: We Have Not Come Here To Take Prisoners. Quote: "Run my dear, from anything that may not strengthen your precious, budding wings. Run like hell my dear, from anyone likely to put a sharp knife into the sacred, tender vision of your beautiful heart."

6. Doyle, Sir Arthur Conan. "A Case of Identity." *The Strand Magazine*, London, UK. 1891. Sherlock Holmes referenced a Haviz quote: "There is danger for him who taketh the tiger cub, and danger also for whoso snatches a delusion from a woman."

7. Doyle, Sir Arthur Conan. *The Valley of Fear.* Quote: "Mediocrity knows nothing higher than itself, but talent instantly recognises genius." *The Strand Magazine*, London, UK. 1914.

8. Paul, Jeremy; Brett, Jeremy. *The Secret of Sherlock Holmes.* Players Press Inc., Studio City, CA, USA. 1991. A British play in 2 acts. Staged at Wyndham's Theatre, London, UK. 1988. A two-hander, it starred Jeremy Brett as Sherlock Holmes and Edward Hardwicke as Doctor Watson.

9. Henry Irving. 1838-1905. Actor-Manager of the Lyceum Theatre, London. Charismatic, sardonic, masterful, considered the most eminent tragedian of his age. The first actor to be knighted. He was also the inspiration for Bram Stoker's *Dracula.* www.theirvingsociety.org/

10. Doyle, Sir Arthur Conan. "A Scandal in Bohemia." Quote: "Grit in a sensitive instrument, or a crack in one of his own high-power lenses, would not be more disturbing than a strong emotion in a nature such as his." *The Strand Magazine*, London, UK. 1891.

11. Shakespeare. *The Life of King Henry V*. Act 1, Prologue. "O for a Muse of fire, that would ascend the brightest heaven of invention, a kingdom for a stage, princes to act, and monarchs to behold the swelling scene!"

12. Wallace, Robert. *The World of Van Gogh: 1853-1890.* Time-Life Library of Art. Vincent Van Gogh quote: "I have walked this earth for thirty years, and, out of gratitude, want to leave some souvenir in the shape of drawings or pictures." Time-Life International, New York, US. 1972.

13. Edward Hardwicke's, and Doctor Watson's birthdays are the seventh of August.

14. The King's Arms Public House. Soho's oldest gay bar. A proud history as a safe space for the LGBTQIA+ community. www.kingsarms-soho.co.uk/london/

15. There are approximately 250–400 Holmesian or Sherlockian literary societies in the world. The largest being The Sherlock

Holmes Society of London and The Japan Sherlock Holmes Club. The US hosts the greatest amount of societies.

16. Roboz, Zsuzsi; Davies, Stan Gebler. *Chichester 10, Portrait of a Decade.* Davis-Poynter Ltd., London, UK. 1971.

17. Jeremy Brett was among the first ensemble, the nucleus of actors who built the National Theatre Company. Laurence Olivier, it's first artistic director, developed the company of actors and theatre professionals that was the budding National Theatre. For its first decade, beginning in 1962, the Chichester Theatre Festival was its incubator. Mr Brett's joyous spirit infused the characters of Bassanio in Jonathan Miller's production of *The Merchant of Venice*; John Tesman opposite Maggie Smith in Ingmar Bergman's *Hedda Gabler*; and Orlando in Clifford Williams's all-male version of *As You Like It*, among many other of the earliest productions that constructed the National Theatre from the ground up. (Ex: *Saint Joan, The Workhouse Donkey, Macbeth, The Rivals, Troilus and Cressida, Edward II, Tartuffe, Romeo and Juliet, Much Ado About Nothing, Love's Labour's Lost, MacRune's Guevara,* et al.) www.nationaltheatre.org.uk/

18. Swift, Jonathan. *Polite Conversation in Three Dialogues.* A complete collection of genteel and ingenious conversation, according to the most polite mode and method now used at court, and in the best companies of England. Quote: "The best doctors in the world are Doctor Diet, Doctor Quiet, and Doctor Merryman." Charles Whittingham & CO at The Chiswick Press. London, UK. 1892. Project Gutenberg. 2019. www.gutenberg.org/

19. "Doctor Theatre will take care of you." Expresses the odd phenomenon that serious debility can occasionally evaporate when one takes the stage.

20. Ali, Hana; Peary, Danny. *Ali on Ali.* Muhammad Ali quote: "Impossible is just a big word thrown around by small men who find it easier to live in the world they've been given than to explore the power they have to change it. Impossible is not a fact.

It's an opinion. Impossible is not a declaration. It's a dare. Impossible is potential. Impossible is temporary. Impossible is nothing." Workman Publishing Company. New York, US. 2018.

21. For Granada TV, Jeremy Brett created the definitive Sherlock Holmes 1984–1994.

NOTE 8: Doctor Watson gave us this insight in "A Scandal in Bohemia" into Holmes's character: *"It was not merely that Holmes changed his costume. His expression, his manner, his very soul seemed to vary with every fresh part that he assumed. The stage lost a fine actor, even as science lost an acute reasoner, when he became a specialist in crime."*

In "The Adventure of the Red Circle," Watson enlightened us: "Holmes was accessible upon the side of flattery, and also, to do him justice, upon the side of kindliness."

With its transition from story to play, *A Toast Darling* was updated and greatly revised. Sherlock was projected into present day London at the request of one of his protégés. Throughout Arthur Conan Doyle's stories, Mr Holmes's playful juggling of truth and lies, was demonstrated in his relationship with the Scotland Yarder's, the villains he brought to justice, and his biographer, Doctor Watson. The only person he cannot baffle was his brother, Mycroft. Sherlock's skill as an incomparable actor was presented in novels: *The Sign of Four* and *The Hound of the Baskervilles*. The Adventure stories: A Scandal in Bohemia, Blue Carbuncle, Naval Treaty, Empty House, Beryl Coronet, Reigate Squires, Charles Augustus Milverton, Dying Detective, Mazarin Stone, and His Last Bow.

Crime is common. Humour is rare.

1. Steele, Frederic Dorr. "Sherlock Holmes in disguise." Arthur Conan Doyle, "The Adventure of Charles Augustus Milverton." Illustration for *Collier's Weekly Magazine*, New York, US. 1904.

A Scandal in Baker Street

1. Van Maële, Martin. Illustration of Irene Adler for "A Scandal in Bohemia." Arthur Conan Doyle. Société d'Édition et de Publications, 1905.
2. Sherlockian.net/ The Portal for the Great Detective. "To Sherlock Holmes she was always The Woman." https://www.sherlockian.net/investigating/ireneadler/
3. Purtanto, Chika Azizah; Solikhah, Ananda Da'watus; Rohmana, Wahyu Indah Mala. "Feminist Character Irene Adler in Sherlock Holmes: A Scandal in Bohemia." A line by line dissection of the character of Irene Adler and Arthur Conan Doyle's short story from a feminist perspective. *Wanastra: Journal Bahasa dan Sastra.* Volume 16 No. 1. Maulana Malik Ibrahim State Islamic University Malang, East Java, Indonesia. 2024.
4. Whitfield, John Humphreys. "Petrarch". Encyclopaedia Britannica. https://www.britannica.com/biography/Petrarch. Serena Professor of Italian Language and Literature, University of Birmingham, England, 1946–74. Author of Petrarch and the Renascence and others. April 15, 2024.
5. Petrarca, Francesco. The Canzoniere (Rerum Vulgarium Fragmenta.) Laura's rhymes in life (1-53.) Atuttascuola. https://www.atuttascuola.it/il-canzoniere-rerum-vulgarium-fragmenta-2/
6. Adventuresses of Sherlock Holmes. "Irene Adler." Excerpted from an article on the website. New York City, US. https://ash-nyc.com/links-and-more/irene-adler/
7. Klinger, Leslie S. *The New Annotated Sherlock Holmes.* Volume 1, page 6. Arthur Conan Doyle. "A Scandal in Bohemia." *W.S. Norton & Company.* New York, US. 2005.
8. Brosnan, Mike. "Irene Adler on Stage." *Ladies, Ladies: The Women in the Life of Sherlock Holmes.* Page 15. Aventine Press, San Diego, CA. 2007.

9. Hardwick, Michael. *Sherlock Holmes. The Carleton Hobbs Collection.* "A Scandal in Bohemia." Carleton Hobbs and Norman Shelley as Sherlock Holmes and Doctor Watson. BBC Radio. London, UK. 1952–1969. This superb radio play is my inspiration for the article.

10. Altabef, Gretchen. *Remarkable Power of Stimulus.* MX Publishing Sherlock Holmes Books. London, UK. 2020. Nine years after "A Scandal in Bohemia," Sherlock Holmes and Irene Adler join forces.

Black Peter's Misplaced Mariners

1. Atherton, Matt. *19th-Century Whaling.* "Sperm whales 'swiftly learned' to evade harpoons in adaptation move to avoid whalers." *Express*, Mar 17, 2021. www.express.co.uk/

2. Doyle, Sir Arthur Conan. "The Adventure Of Black Peter." *Collier's Weekly Magazine.* 1904.

3. Ellis, Richard. *Men And Whales.* Alfred A. Knopf, Inc., New York, 1991.

4. New Bedford Whaling Museum. 18 Johnny Cake Hill, New Bedford, MA 02740. www.whalingmuseum.org/learn/research-topics/whaling-history/whales-and-hunting/

5. Ash, Christopher. *Whaler's Eye.* New York: Macmillan, 1962; London: George Allen & Unwin, 1964. Modern whaling narrative of the British floating-factory whale-ship Balaena.

6. Elliott, Sir Gerald. *Whaling 1937-1967: The International Control of Whale Stocks.* Kendall Monograph #10. Sharon, Massachusetts, 1997.

7. Tønnessen, J. N.; and A.O. Johnson. *The History of Modern Whaling.* Translated by R.I. Christophersen. Berkeley and Los Angeles: University of California Press. 1982.

8. Becket, Samuel. *Waiting for Godot.* Grove Press, New York. 1954.

The Adventure of Black Peter
By Sir Arthur Conan Doyle

1. Doyle, Sir Arthur Conan. "The Adventure Of Black Peter." Illustrated by Frederic Dorr Steele for the cover of *Collier's Weekly Magazine*. 1904.

NOTE 10: "The Adventure of Black Peter" was first published as a short story in *Collier's Magazine*, New York, USA, in February 1904 and in *The Strand Magazine*, London, UK, in March 1904. This is Sir Arthur Conan Doyle's 33rd Sherlock Holmes mystery of sixty in total. It was collected in book form with other stories in *The Return of Sherlock Holmes*.

Notes For Curious and Author Page Illustrations

1. Steele, Frederic Dorr. "The one thing I don't know about it, you're going to tell me now, Holmes announced calmly." Arthur Conan Doyle, "The Adventure of the Mazarin Stone." Illustration for *Hearst's International Magazine*, New York, US. 1921.

2. Steele, Frederic Dorr. Illustration of Sherlock Holmes. Arthur Conan Doyle, "The Adventure of the Golden Pince-Nez." *Collier's Magazine*, New York, US. 1904.

*Frederic Dorr Steele's illustration of Sherlock Holmes for
"The Adventure of the Golden Pince-Nez."*

Author Page

Gretchen Altabef is an award-winning author of new Sherlock Holmes mysteries, sci-fi, and historical stories. Her books brim with imagination and a news reporter's excitement for the true history of the day.

These Scattered Houses brings a wounded Holmes to New York at the end of his 'great hiatus' to face a Goliath unlike any he has before.

Remarkable Power Of Stimulus follows immediately. Cupid gets involved during the investigation of a gruesome London murder. Watson falls for a suffragist and Holmes seizes his second chance with *The* Woman.

Five Miles Of Country continues the Rachel Holmes trilogy. Summoned to New York, Holmes solves a murder in Thomas Edison's film studio. While Mrs Irene Adler-Holmes confronts prejudice on Broadway.

The Keys Of Death is a genesis story of the world's most famous address, No. 221B Baker Street. Twentysomethings Holmes and Watson set up a new and vulnerable detective agency in Mrs Hudson's first-floor flat. Together, the three companions solve the murder of Mr James Hudson.

Far & Wide is a collection of Ms Altabef's short stories and one play.

She is a member of The Adventuresses of Sherlock Holmes, The Sherlock Holmes Society of London, The John H. Watson Society, and The ACD Society.

Her website: featuresofinterest.com.